"Good afternoon, Captain Ricardo, Captain Smirk," Dacron said with a polite nod to each of them as he entered the room. Lowering his head, Smirk pressed his fist harder against his mouth and managed to waggle his fingers at Dacron. His shoulders shook.

Forced to acknowledge Dacron's presence, Ricardo stared, aghast, as if he'd just seen Marley's ghost again. His voice faint, almost plaintive, Ricardo inquired, "Dacron, why are you wearing . . . a *dress?*"

"You had asked me to assume an investigator's persona in my search for the missing crewmembers," Dacron explained. "I am tired of playing Sherlock Holmes. This time I have decided to take on the identity of Nancy Drew."

STAR WRECK 6
Geek Space Nine
A PARODY

D0710181

St. Martin's Paperbacks Titles by
Leah Rewolinski

STAR WRECK 6

GEEK SPACE NINE

An extraterrestrial example
of extreme silliness

by
LEAH REWOLINSKI

ILLUSTRATIONS BY
HARRY TRUMBORE

A 2M COMMUNICATIONS LTD. PRODUCTION

ST. MARTIN'S PAPERBACKS

Star Wreck is an unauthorized parody of the *Star Trek* television and motion picture series, the *Star Trek: The Next Generation* television series, and the *Star Trek: Deep Space Nine* television series. None of the individuals or companies associated with these series or with any merchandise based upon these series, has in any way sponsored, approved, endorsed or authorized this book.

Published by arrangement with the author

STAR WRECK 6: GEEK SPACE NINE

Copyright © 1994 by Leah Rewolinski.

Cover illustration by Bob Larkin.
Text illustrations copyright © 1994 by Harry Trumbore.

ISBN: 0-312-95223-6

Printed in the United States of America

St. Martin's Paperbacks edition/April 1994

10 9 8 7 6 5 4 3 2

To all the dogs I've loved before

Contents

Contents

Prologue

1 In the beginning, Westerns ruled the heavens and the earth. [2]And the universe of television was without form, and void of futuristic ideas. [3]So RODenberry said, "What the world needs now is a 'Wagon Train' to the stars."

4 And RODenberry said, "Let us create a captain in our own image, and other crewmembers from every race and creed among humankind." And RODenberry saw that it was berry good. [5]Thus was born The Original Series[A], which did last for 79 episodes; and its disciples remain faithful unto this day.

6 Then RODenberry said, "It is not good for my crew to be alone in syndication. I will make a helpmeet for them." [7]In this way did the Next Generation come into being. [8]RODenberry said, "Let us create a captain in our present image, and a first officer in the image of our young adulthood, and a dorky ensign in the image of our adolescence." And so it was. [9]Again RODenberry surveyed all that he had made and found that it was berry good. [10]The disciples, except those who hated the guts of the dorky ensign, agreed. [11]In this way the numbers of the followers grew till they were countless as the grains of sand.

12 Then somebody said, "Lo, this is an exceedingly prof-

[A]Or *The Old Series*

1

itable franchise which bears repeating. [13]Except that this time the starship shall become a space station. [14]And drama shall become melodrama. [15]And characters shall become caricatures." [16]Thus was born Geek Space Nine. [17]When its broadcast days came to pass, everybody rested; verily, the stories did put them to sleep.

18 All this was done to fulfill the words of the prophets who had prophesied: "What goes around comes around," for once again the universe was without form and void of ideas.

1

Space, the
Finite Frontier

I T WASN'T ONE of Commander Bungeeman Crisco's better
mornings.

He was startled out of a sound sleep at 0600 hours
by a blast shaking his space station, Geek Space Nine.
Crisco donned his Starfreak uniform and stumbled sleepily
down the Promenade, a two-story mall that had been en-
closed to protect shoppers from snow, wind, rain, and the
vacuum of space.

Halfway down the Promenade, he found the blast site.
Acrid smoke lingered over the heads of curious onlookers.
A gaping hole was all that remained of what had been a
lizard-skin-lingerie boutique during the days of Carcinogen occupation.

Crisco zigzagged through the shop, sidestepping twisted
pieces of metal, shards of glass, and remnants of peekaboo
nighties. Finally he stood beside Smiles O'Brine, his fix-it
chief, who was examining the rubble for clues.

"Definitely a Bridgeoran bomb," O'Brine concluded.
"Standard terrorist issue. You want me to file a report,
Commander?"

"That won't be necessary, Chief," said Crisco. "Perhaps
I'll have a word with Major Vera about this later." O'Brine
nodded, politely allowing Crisco to maintain the fiction

3

that this time he might actually discipline his second-in-command, Major Vera Obese.

Major Vera was a former Bridgeoran terrorist who now served as liaison between the federation—which maintained Crisco's space station—and her nearby home world, Badger. Crisco wished she'd be more fastidious about choosing a place to practice her bombing skills.

Without proof that this was Vera's handiwork, Crisco didn't dare risk her wrath by questioning her, and issuing a reprimand was out of the question. Bridgeorans were still hyper-touchy from the days of occupation by the Carcinogens. And even though they were free of Carcinogen oppression, their society still rewarded defiance and violence. For every bomb that Major Vera set off in a populated area, she earned another credit toward her B.A.—Bridgeoran Attitude.

As Crisco left the storefront and continued down the Promenade, he saw Chief Medical Officer Dr. Julio Brassiere walking a few steps ahead of him. Crisco noticed something different about Brassiere and felt a stab of displeasure. *There's another example of the lack of respect Starfreak commands on this station*, Crisco thought. Someone had taped a "Kick Me" note to Dr. Brassiere's back.

Crisco followed Brassiere into Quirk's, a Ferengi-owned bar. For weeks, Crisco had been looking forward to trying the champagne brunch served at Quirk's on Ferengi holidays, and today happened to be Earbor Day.

Normally Crisco tried to set a good example by avoiding Quirk's bar, a drinking and gambling establishment which also offered the delights of a virtual-reality brothel known as the Hollowsweets. However, at this hour the place was so quiet that few citizens would notice Crisco's presence.

Crisco stepped up to the buffet table, but before he could take a plate, Dr. Brassiere stopped him. "I'm sorry, Com-*mahn*der," Brassiere said in his tea-and-crumpets accent, "but I'm afraid you'll have to breakfast somewhere else."

Crisco wished Vera would be more fastidious about choosing a place to practice her bombing skills.

Brassiere taped a sign atop the steam tray of scrambled whippoorwill eggs. It read "Closed by Order of Starfreak Board of Health."

In a flash, Quirk appeared at their side. "What's this?" he demanded, his oversized Ferengi ears twitching as he sensed a threat to his income.

"Your buffet may present a hazard to public health, Quirk," Dr. Brassiere said. "I'm shutting it down as a precaution until Security Chief Dodo is found. You know he hasn't been seen since the last time he went into his gelatinous resting state, don't you?"

Crisco broke in, "What does that have to do with shutting down Quirk's buffet?"

Brassiere explained, "There's a rumor going around that somehow Dodo has gotten mixed up in the oatmeal."

"Lies, vicious lies," Quirk sneered. "I'll bet that new McDoogle's on the Promenade started this rumor just so they could sell more Egg McShakes. Business is slow enough in here without you scaring everybody off, Brassiere." Quirk turned to Crisco. "Commander, can't I set aside the oatmeal and keep the rest of the buffet open?"

Crisco surveyed the steam tables. "I suppose so," he replied, turning away from the food with a sigh; for some reason he'd lost his appetite for breakfast. He told Quirk, "Don't forget, we have a meeting this morning in about thirty minutes," and walked away.

"I'll be there," Quirk replied.

Crisco strolled over to the Sloperations Command Center. This was the nerve center of the space station, which on the whole had an overabundance of nerve. *Now, if it only had a heart*, Crisco thought, *and a brain*.

Major Vera stood in the center of the Center, facing the Main Viewscreen, which showed a starship captain seeking permission to dock at the station.

"What's the magic word?" Vera demanded.

The captain looked exasperated. "I don't know," she said. "I just want to take on food and medical supplies for my passengers. They're refugees from the meteor shower on Dilettante-4."

Vera slammed her hand on the countertop. "Ha!" she shouted. "You call that a hard-luck story? Let me tell you about the years of Carcinogen occupation of Badger. . . ."

Crisco trudged up the no-frills metal steps to Level 1 1/2, schlepped through the door to his office, and sank into the chair behind his desk. A moment later, his personal Viewscreen beeped at him and displayed the words "Incoming message." He pressed the "answer" button, and Admiral Troy Gogetter appeared on the screen.

"Bungee, baby," said Admiral Gogetter. "What's shakin'?"

"Hello, Admiral," Crisco replied. Mindful that Gogetter was director of marketing for this sector and therefore held the fate of the entire station in his hands, Crisco could never bring himself to match the admiral's level of informality. "What can I do for you?"

"Hang on a sec," Gogetter replied. He began speaking into the phone receiver cradled between his shoulder and his left ear. "Marv, you gotta understand, you can't treat the talent that way," he said into the receiver. "Marv . . . Marv . . . listen to me . . ."

As Gogetter held the phone away from his ear, Crisco could hear Marv's tirade crackling through the line. Gogetter shrugged and said in an aside, "He won't listen." Crisco attempted a sympathetic smile.

"Marv," Gogetter cut in, "can you hold on for just a second?" Gogetter stabbed the "hold" button on the base of the phone, then reached into a white paper bag on his desk and pulled out a jelly roll. He bit into it, bleated a loud "Mmrrrzzhh!" and clutched his mouth. Grabbing the wastebasket from the floor next to his desk, Gogetter spit the mouthful of jelly roll into it.

"Mandy!" he hollered. A secretary appeared at his side in an instant. "How many times do I have to tell you not to buy these sweet rolls with boysenberry filling?" Gogetter

Crisco schlepped through the door to his office and
sank into the chair behind his desk.

scolded. "Get me some spring water to rinse out with."
Mandy disappeared. Gogetter turned back to his Viewscreen.

"Anyway, Bungeeman," he said, as if continuing a conversation, "how's our hot new thing?"

"Uh—I beg your pardon?" Crisco stumbled.

"The space station, baby, the space station," Gogetter said. From the top drawer of his desk, he pulled out a pair of scissors. "We're a little worried about your hot property, Bunge," said Gogetter. With one hand he held up a mirror; with the other, he snipped at his bangs with the shears. Hair fell onto his desktop.

"We've got a lot riding on your three-ringed circus floating out there next to the wormhole," Gogetter continued. "People are saying you're not living up to your billing, and alien traffic is way down. *Way* down," he repeated, sweeping the hair into a pile and wafting it toward the wastebasket.

Mandy appeared at his side and handed him a bottle of spring water. "Do you want me to empty that wastebasket for you, sir?" she asked. "It's getting awfully full."

"No," he said. "Nobody touches this wastebasket but me, understand?" He took a swallow from the water bottle, then faced his Viewscreen again. "So, Bungeeman, your station has gotta live up to the hype. Don't leave us standing here with our nacelles dragging around our ankles, you know what I mean?"

"Certainly, Admir—" Crisco began; but Gogetter had already signed off.

Crisco's pulse hammered in his ears, and he considered leaving the office for a while to let off steam. *I could go to the gym for a bodybuilding workout on those Carcinogen torture racks O'Brine converted to weight-lifting machines*, he thought. But then he remembered the early meeting he'd scheduled with Quirk; it was now just a few minutes away.

Crisco mused over the irony that Quirk, regarded as one

I could go to the gym for a workout on those
Carcinogen torture racks, Crisco thought.

of the station's most prominent citizens, was a kingpin in the Ferengi underworld. Not that anyone was intimidated by the Ferengi—a race that looked like a Stephen King version of Howdy Doody—but their fondness for petty crime made it hard to keep order on the space station.

A moment later, the doors from the Command Center whooshed open. Major Vera ushered Quirk into the office with Bridgeoran finesse, tossing him like a rag doll. Quirk sailed through the air, hit the far wall, and slid down to the floor.

"What a woman," Quirk marveled, shaking his head with a dazed look of admiration as Vera exited, briskly brushing her hands together over another job well done.

Quirk dragged himself over to a chair in front of Crisco's desk. "You wanted to see me about something, Commander?" he asked.

"It's this security report from Dodo," Crisco began, holding up a piece of paper. "He says you—"

"I didn't do it," Quirk protested.

"Quirk, at least wait until I read you the charges."

"Well, whatever happened, I have an alibi," Quirk maintained. "I was in a Hollowsweet at the time with some of my ... er, escorts. They'll testify for me."

"Will you let me finish?" Crisco said. He glanced at the paper. "Dodo says you've violated Ordinance 433.222b of the federation legal code by selling lewd earmuffs." Crisco set down the report and added, "Look, Quirk, I know ears are an erogenous zone for the Ferengi—"

"We prefer the term 'earogenous zone,' " Quirk interjected.

Crisco went on, "Whatever. I don't care what you people do in private, but you can't keep selling these earmuffs openly. It sets a bad example."

"But they were in a plain brown wrapper," Quirk countered. "It clearly stated 'for use as a marital aid only' and 'must be eighteen or over to purchase.' Besides, you let

Major Vera wear that chain ornament on her ear all the time. Is she into bondage or what?"

"Don't be ridiculous. You know the Bridgeoran ear chain has religious significance," Crisco argued. "The custom has nothing to do with their recreational practices." *Besides, I don't have the nerve to ask her not to wear it while she's on duty*, he thought. *She might slug me.*

"How about if I take the earmuffs out of the vending machines and only sell them from behind the counter?" Quirk suggested.

"Quirk . . ."

"Restraint of trade is not taken lightly in my circle," Quirk added with a hint of menace. "Remember, I have friends in low places."

"Oh, all right." Crisco seemed weary of the argument. "You can sell them from behind the counter." Quirk grinned and walked out the door. "But take them off the mannequins on your balcony!" Crisco called after him.

No sooner had the doors shut behind Quirk than another call came in on the personal Viewscreen atop the desk. Crisco was startled to see the face of the caller. It was James T. Smirk, captain of the original USS *Endocrine*.

Oddly, Smirk wasn't a teen as he'd been when Crisco met him; now he looked older than Crisco. *Something must have gone wrong with the Fountain of Youth water that was holding back the years for him and his crew*, Crisco thought, recognizing Smirk's adult face from an old Starfreak photo he'd once seen.

"I told you never to call me here!" Crisco hissed at the Viewscreen. "What do you want?" Nervously he glanced at the door as if fearing that someone from the Sloperations Center would walk in on this conversation.

"It doesn't matter anymore, Bunge," replied Smirk, steadily gazing at him from the screen of the viewer. "The whole gig is up, anyway."

An icy chill zipped through Crisco's liver. "What do you mean?"

"Starfreak Command kicked my crew out of our Juven Isle Amusement Park and took over the Fountain of Youth for themselves," Smirk said. "We're back on our ship again."

Crisco gripped the edges of the Viewscreen in disbelief. Smirk seemed mildly amused at the effect his announcement had on Crisco. "Hadn't you noticed that we'd stopped sending you fountain water?" Smirk asked.

Numbly, Crisco shook his head. Lately he'd been so busy trying to keep order at his crumbling space station that he hadn't kept track of the profit from his illicit sales of fountain water.

Smirk continued, "Starfreak left my crew just enough water to gradually wean ourselves back to the age we were before. That wasn't such a big deal for me, you understand," he added, glancing at the mirror next to his desk as he ran a comb through his toupee, "but my senior officers are having a rough time on re-entry, so to speak. I'm the only one fit for Bridge duty. The rest of them are all in Sick Bay."

Crisco blurted out, "Does Starfreak know about the supply of Fountain of Youth water you'd been diverting to me?"

"No," Smirk replied. "I kept you out of it. You owe me one, pal."

"Thanks," Crisco sighed. As his momentary panic ebbed away, he noticed that Smirk's usually mellow expression had begun to look a little perturbed around the edges. *Perhaps I'd better smooth things over*, Crisco thought. "Gee, I'm sorry about all of this," he offered. "I know you and your crew thought you were pretty well set for life when you controlled the fountain."

"Yes, we did," Smirk said, his jaw thrust forward. "And I'd like to know how Starfreak found out they were getting only a fraction of the fountain's output through their transplanetary pipeline."

"Wha—?" The implication hit Crisco like a Kringle

cream pie in the face. "Are you saying that I squealed?"

"You tell me," Smirk countered. "You and I were the only ones who knew what was going on. And I know *I* didn't tell them."

As indignation flooded Crisco, he felt sure of himself for the first time since Smirk had called. *All right*, he thought, *if you want a fight, I'll give you one. I've had plenty of practice since taking over command of this place. All we ever do around here is fight.*

"Listen, Jimbo," Crisco began, deliberately using a nickname he knew Smirk hated, "I couldn't have spilled the beans about our agreement because I've been too busy lately to bother with office politics. First, the admiral who oversees this sector is on my back because the traffic among our sleazeball tourists has been way down lately. Second, my Bridgeoran first officer and some of the other outstanding role models on this station instigate brawls nearly every day, causing no end of trouble for me and my security chief."

Crisco was building up quite a froth of righteous anger. It had become his chronic response to the goings-on at the station. With veins popping from his forehead, lips pursed, and a voice icy with disdain, he could have passed for a high school principal.

"And that's not all," Crisco went on. "I'm dealing with constant warfare between rival alien gangs and wondering if I should get my son Joke away from all this, maybe send him to a Catholic school on the other side of the wormhole. I haven't had time in the last six months even to think about the deal you and I made, much less to go squealing to Starfreak Command about it. Do I make myself clear?"

Maddeningly, Smirk refused to rise to the bait. "Gee, Bunge, it sounds like you don't like it there," he observed blandly. "I guess you won't mind, then, if Admiral Gogetter relieves you of command."

Again Crisco felt himself being tipped off-balance. "Why would Gogetter do that?" he countered.

"If he found out you'd been taking a cut from their Fountain of Youth water," Smirk said, "and realized you can't live up to your squeaky-clean billing anymore, he'd strip you of command faster than you could say 'parametric subspace flatulence sensor.'"

"You're not about to tell him about our deal," Crisco said, trying to keep his voice steady, "not while there's still the little matter of Captain Ricardo's crew being stuck in the nursing home." Crisco paused, letting the implication sink in: Gogetter's bosses in the High Command thought it was Smirk's crew in the nursing home, living out a mandatory retirement sentence. Crisco added, "I wouldn't want to have to set them straight, but if you push me—"

"That 'little matter' has taken care of itself," Smirk interrupted. "Ricardo's crew was released from the nursing home yesterday."

A strangled sound escaped Crisco's throat.

Smirk went on, "It seems as though nobody at Starfreak Command cares whether there was a mixup or not. They want both my crew and Ricardo's on duty, and they're all hot and bothered about getting us to start some urgent new mission.

"Ricardo and I are meeting this morning to discuss it," Smirk said, frowning at the thought. "Ricardo has Starfreak's paperwork with the details. Right now all I know is that our crewmembers are supposed to give your space station people some kind of career counseling. I expect that our ships will arrive at your docking ring in a day or two." Crisco wilted in resignation.

"Better start getting that junky station of yours into shape, Commander," Smirk said. In the halting speech he frequently used to make a dramatic point, he concluded, "I expect you to make sure my visit . . . is . . . very . . . comfortable. Smirk out."

Once Smirk's image disappeared from the Viewscreen, Crisco felt an energizing surge of anger. *So the honchos*

of Starfreak think we need career advice, do they?
Straightening his shoulders, he decided to head for the
Promenade, where he could find someone to pick on. But
as he pushed away from the desk, the stapler on the far
corner caught his eye.

The top of the stapler was chattering up and down as it
made tiny gasps: "Aah ... aaah ... aaaahhh...." With a
final cry—"Aaaachoooo!"—the top of the stapler flung itself open, and its inner bar sprang forward.

Crisco caught on. "All right, Dodo," Crisco said. "You
might as well come out now."

The stapler dissolved into a mercurylike blob, and the
blob grew, then reassembled itself on the desktop as Dodo,
Crisco's shape-shifting chief of security.

"You really ought to see a doctor about that dust allergy," Crisco said, obviously trying to stifle a grin. "It's
blown your cover in a lot of covert operations lately."

"Hmmph," Dodo sniffed. "I wouldn't have this problem
if you people would keep your offices clean." Dodo shifted
position and grimaced, noticing that he was sitting on
Crisco's letter opener. He climbed off the desktop, commenting, "So Starfreak is sending its high and mighty
captains to teach us some manners out here on the frontier, hmm?"

"I'm afraid so," Crisco said. "And as you no doubt
overheard, Smirk's got the goods on me, so it pays for us
to keep everybody happy."

"Do you want me to round up the usual suspects?" Dodo
inquired. "Make the streets of Geek Space Nine safe for
the starship crews and the cushy life to which they're
accustomed?" He somehow managed to look menacing
despite his doughy expression.

Ignoring the sarcasm in Dodo's voice, Crisco ordered,
"Just make sure the troublemakers stay in line, and try to
see that no fights break out. Keep a close eye on their
ringleader. You know who I mean."

Dodo nodded. They both glanced through the glass

panels of the door and studied that ringleader, who stood in the center of the Sloperations area; Major Vera had drawn a chalk line on the floor and was daring one of her co-workers to step over it.

"Let's get down to work, shall we?" Capt. Jean-Lucy Ricardo invited.

"If we must," conceded Capt. Smirk.

The two of them sat in the Ready Room of Capt. Ricardo's ship as both their ships traveled toward Geek Space Nine. Smirk's crewmembers had managed to pull themselves together and adjust to their newly-aged bodies well enough to manage his ship. Ricardo's crewmembers were also going through a break-in curve, reassuming their previous shipboard responsibilities after months of vegging in the Vacant Attic Nursing Home. They'd been kicked out onto the sidewalk by their caretakers with a sentimental farewell: "Starfreak Command says you've loafed long enough."

Capt. Ricardo indicated a folder full of papers and said, "I've studied Starfreak's objectives for this mission. Would you like to read them yourself?"

"No, thanks," said Smirk. "Just give me the nitty gritty."

Ricardo began, "The residents of Geek Space Nine seem to be suffering from a mysterious personality ailment. For lack of a better term, Starfreak simply refers to it as 'dullimia.'

"The station's key officers and prominent citizens are so shallow and predictable that they're putting visitors to sleep," Ricardo said. "At first Starfreak suspected an outbreak of sleeping sickness, but investigators found that this drowsiness is just a reaction to the syndrome.

"The station's air quality was—let me see here..." Ricardo referred to a statistical document in the folder. "Ah, yes, here it is: 'BanalMeter tests of the station's breathable atmosphere reveal 148 parts per million of hackney molecules.' So Starfreak engineers installed Glade Idea Fresheners on all the air ducts. However, that tactic only increased the general level of aggression. People spend a lot of time shouting at each other, but even their conflicts are tiresome."

Smirk interjected, "I'd heard that aliens have been avoiding the station. Now I know why."

"Yes," Ricardo said, "and that has Starfreak Command very worried, because the station is supposed to provide a key strategic position for the federation. After all, it's right next to a wormhole leading to the Gummi Quadrant.

"According to Starfreak, stagnation affects every aspect of society on Geek Space Nine. Even its currency is based on a soporific—gold-pressed laudanum."

Smirk squirmed in his chair. "Look, Jean-Lucy, you know I'm allergic to boredom. Are you sure my crew has to get mixed up in this?"

Ricardo nodded. "Starfreak's staff psychiatrists believe that it will be a full-time project for both of our crews. We've got to coach the residents of Geek Space Nine into a state of full character dimensionality."

Smirk looked puzzled. "Character dimensionality?"

"Yes. You know—depth of character . . . believability . . . texture . . . subtlety. Multiple motivations, conflicting emotions, lovable foibles and faults. Realistic traits and inconsistencies. Something people can latch onto, so they care whether you live or die when you're confronted with some far-fetched catastrophe."

"Ah, dimensionality," Smirk said. "Gotcha. My crew is loaded with it. Heck, we ought to be. We've been working at it for—well, let's not go into how many years we've been working at it. So how should we approach this thing?"

"Starfreak Command has explicitly outlined our mission parameters," Ricardo said. "You and I are to assign the appropriate personnel from our crews to coach the station's key people. They're to be matched by job function and personality." Ricardo handed Smirk a manila folder marked *Starfreak Command Report: Geek Space Nine Per-*

sonnel, Key Citizens, and Assorted Hangers-On.

Smirk pulled out the stack of personnel papers, each with a photo attached, and began leafing through them. "Commander Bungeeman Crisco..." he read aloud, studying the pictures as he went, "...his son Joke.... Major Vera Obese...hmm, what's with her uniform? Is she wearing foam shoulder pads?"

"That's the Bridgeoran chip on her shoulder," Ricardo explained. "I read about it elsewhere in the report."

"She looks ornery," Smirk observed. He continued to glance at the papers, thinking aloud. "A Ferengi bartender named Quirk—seems to have a bit of a problem with mid-riff bulge...his nephew, Eggnog...and Dr. Julio Brassiere. Look at him—probably worked his way through med school by modeling on the side." Smirk flipped to the next page. "Huh—what's this?"

Ricardo identified the picture Smirk held up. "That is Dodo, the station's chief of security."

"So *that's* what became of the Pillsbury Doughboy," Smirk said. "I always wondered."

"He's a shape-shifter," Ricardo explained. "He hasn't quite mastered human physiology."

"I used to know a shape-shifter," Smirk said. "She helped me escape from prison on an ice planet. We still keep in touch. Every Christmas I send her a box of cigars." Smirk picked up the next picture and asked, "Wasn't this one of your crewmembers?"

Ricardo nodded. "Smiles O'Brine used to be my trans-porter chief. He transferred over to Geek Space Nine to take a more challenging job. Unfortunately, I hear that his wife Kookoo isn't too happy living on the space station."

"Gee, I can't imagine why," Smirk wisecracked, "when she's got such a fun bunch of people to hang around with."

Setting aside O'Brine's picture, Smirk uncovered the last report and nearly jumped out of his chair. There were three shots of this officer: one in an evening gown; the second in a bikini cut high on the thigh; and the third a head shot, with her face makeupped to the porcelain perfection worthy of a *Vogue* cover.

"Hoo-aah! Get a load of her!" Smirk panted, clutching the edges of the picture. " 'Lieutenant Jazzy Fax, science officer,' " he read from the label. "Now that is one classy dame!"

"She happens to be a Thrill," Ricardo said.

"One of those symbiont beings that takes on a new host body every so often?" said Smirk, unfazed by the news. He seemed about to drown in drool.

"That's right," Ricardo said, adding in a spoilsport tone of voice, "and her previous host was an old man."

Smirk looked taken aback for a moment, but then his eyes were irresistibly drawn to Fax's classic cheekbones. "Well, nobody's perfect," he reasoned.

Ricardo pulled out a list. "For the person-to-person coaching assignments, I've taken the liberty of matching up the members of our crews with the station's personnel according to Starfreak's guidelines," he said. "I hope you don't mind my going ahead with this."

"Not a bit," Smirk replied. "That's less work for me. Let's hear 'em."

Ricardo consulted his list. "Naturally, you and I will counsel Commander Crisco. Our second-in-commands—your Mr. Smock and my Commander Piker—will work with Major Vera. My chief of security, Wart, is matched with Dodo. Our medical personnel, Dr. Lynyrd McCaw and Dr. Beverage Flusher, will be mentors for Dr. Julio Brassiere."

"Dr. Brassiere? Are you sure Dr. Flusher won't resent having to work with a colleague who's prettier than she is?" Smirk wondered.

Ricardo raised his eyebrows at Smirk and went on. "Your engineer, Montgomery Ward Snot, and mine, Georgie LaForgery, are teamed with Smiles O'Brine, who does a lot of repair work on the station. My bartender, Guano,

"She happens to be a Thrill, one of those symbiont beings that takes on a new host body every so often."

will be assigned to work with Quirk, the Ferengi, in his bar."

Ricardo cleared his throat before going on. "At this point, the job categories get a little vague," he said. "The matchups are more intuitive than objective. Perhaps you can help me assign labels to these groups."

"Shoot," Smirk responded.

Ricardo began, "I've matched Counselor Dee Troit and your Communications Officer Yoohoo with Lieutenant Jazzy Fax. . . ."

"Fripperies," Smirk judged, and Ricardo wrote this on the chart in the column marked "category."

"Then there are your officers Zulu and Checkout, whose duties seem . . ." Ricardo hesitated, " . . . that is, the two of them appear to be rather . . ."

"Superfluous?" Smirk supplied.

Ricardo nodded, adding, "They don't have any counterparts at the station."

"Write 'at-large' in the assignment column," Smirk suggested.

Ricardo made the entry, then said, "Westerly Flusher, who has returned to my ship from Starfreak Academy Film School, seems to have a lot in common with Commander Crisco's son, Joke."

"Dweebs," Smirk judged.

"And the final pairing is Wart's son, Smartalecsander, and Quirk's nephew, Eggnog."

"Just call them 'boys from dysfunctional families,' " Smirk directed.

"Also, my second officer Dacron has no counterpart, either, since there are no androids on the space station," Ricardo said. "I was hoping he could tag along with us, if you don't mind . . ." Ricardo tugged at his tunic nervously, " . . . that is, if you no longer resent him for . . . ah . . ."

"For the time he snatched Deanna Troit out of my arms and made her break our engagement? Not at all," Smirk breezed. "Seeing Dacron on TV a few months ago did wonders for my grudge. You remember—he was performing as an Elvis wannabe. There's nothing like watching a rival make a fool of himself to help you forgive and forget.

"Besides, as far as I'm concerned, Deanna is yesterday's mashed potatoes," Smirk added. Again he gazed at the composite photo of Jazzy Fax. "Now that's what I call a *superior* officer."

Commander Crisco's face appeared on the Viewscreen of each Bridge as the two *Endocrines* approached the space station. "Welcome to Geek Space Nine," Crisco greeted the captains.

"I'm afraid I'll have to ask you to park a few kilometers away from our docking bays," Crisco said. "They're out of order this week. And your crewmembers won't be able to UltraFax over here, because our Shipping and Receiving pads are broken, too. Smiles O'Brine promised me he'd get to both repairs as soon as he finishes fixing the photocopier in Dodo's office."

After the ships maneuvered into parking spaces, Capt. Smirk boarded a shuttle and swung over to the shuttlebay of the other ship to give Capt. Ricardo and Dacron a ride. Ricardo climbed aboard the shuttle immediately, but Dacron was nowhere in sight.

"Dacron will be along in a minute," Ricardo told Smirk. "He's taking a benzocaine bath in Sick Bay. Some crewmember played another practical joke on him this morning, putting extract of poison oak in his glass of WD-40 at breakfast."

Once Dacron arrived, Smirk maneuvered the shuttle out of the ship and toward the space station. The officers gazed through the shuttle windshield at the ungainly structure that towered before them, its three pylons curling inward like the claws of a dead crab washed up on the beach.

"Not the coziest lodging, is it?" Ricardo mused.

"Hmmm," Smirk murmured. "It looks a bit like a Kringle IUD."

Ricardo winced at the image this evoked and replied, "I wouldn't know."

"The design *is* similar," Dacron chimed in, "but careful examination will reveal the absence of the sharp hooks that appear on the projectile ends of the Kringle—"

"That's enough, Dacron," Capt. Ricardo ordered.

The station's shuttlebay personnel gave them clearance to enter. As Smirk made the approach, Ricardo offered a last-minute instruction. "When Starfreak's Human Resources people gave me the assignment, they suggested that we play down the need for career counseling among the station's personnel," Ricardo said. "It's a touchy subject here, exaggerated by the residents' high aggression level and the prevailing Bridgeoran attitude."

"Outposts do tend to attract prickly types," Smirk observed.

"So even though they've been told in vague terms that they need counseling," Ricardo continued, "the residents must be allowed to save face. We're supposed to say simply that we've come on a 'fact-finding mission.'"

Smirk piloted the shuttle to a stop in the bay, checked his hair in the rearview mirror, and climbed out the rear door after Ricardo and Dacron. Commander Crisco stood there waiting to meet them.

Tension crackled in the air as the four stood beside the shuttle and exchanged greetings. The expressions of Smirk, Ricardo, and Crisco broadcast their emotions.

"Nice to meet you, Commander Crisco," said Capt. Smirk with a stern look that said, *Remember, we'd agreed to pretend we've never met*.

"The pleasure's all mine," Crisco replied with a conciliatory smile that begged, *Let's be pals, and please don't ever mention to Starfreak that deal we had with the fountain water*.

"How do you do, Commander Crisco," said Ricardo, offering his hand and smiling as if to say, *I'm willing to forgive you for mistakenly sending my crew to the nursing home.*

"Captain." Nodding curtly, Crisco ignored Ricardo's attempt at a handshake, his expression shouting, *Big deal— that doesn't make up for killing my wife in the attack you led on our ship when you were Lowcutie, a Bored.*

Only Dacron was immune from the tension. As he waited for Ricardo to introduce him to Crisco, he wondered, *Will I get off duty in time to watch today's episode of "As the Starship Turns"?*

When they had finished the formalities, an awkward silence settled in. Ricardo attempted to break it. "So! Here we are at last on Geek Space Nine for our fault-finding mission."

A deep frown creased Crisco's face, and Ricardo amended, "Er, I mean our *fact*-finding mission."

"Commander Crisco," Dacron said, and for once Ricardo was happy to hear the android open his mouth, "will we be able to tour your arboretum?" Dacron scratched his chest. "I am particularly interested in seeing the succulent plants and cactus. Perhaps a sprig of aloe vera would alleviate my rash."

"I'm sorry, Mr. Dacron," Crisco replied, "but you must have been misinformed. We don't have an arboretum here, and we've got no cactus plants to speak of."

"Mmmm. I see," Dacron reflected. "I envisioned a variety of spiny plants when Captain Smirk said your outpost has a climate favoring a prickly orientation."

Capt. Ricardo, already flushed with embarrassment from his previous gaffe, now looked like he wanted to crawl under the shuttlecraft. Crisco gave Smirk a nasty stare; Smirk returned the stare with a half-smile that taunted, *Are you gonna try to make something of it?*

Dacron went on, "I recently read a fascinating article on cacti in the *Rational Geographic*. It said that the Spiny-Leaved Vindictive Yucca can ensnare a herd of longhorn cattle with its thorns, then use its caustic juices to digest the entire herd within a week. There is also the intriguing Miser Cactus, which can go without water for up to seventeen years in the desert but dies in a home greenhouse if left untended over a long weekend. In addition, the . . ."

"Captain Ricardo, may I speak to you for a minute?" Crisco asked with a pained expression. Without waiting for a reply, he steered Ricardo by the elbow toward a far corner as Dacron babbled on.

"Captain, your android is giving me a headache," Crisco said. "And as you'll discover when you meet my medical officer, this station already has its quota of blabbermouths."

"Of course, of course," Ricardo hurriedly assented. "I'll keep him out of your way." They returned to Smirk and Dacron.

Ricardo interrupted Dacron's monologue and took him aside, saying, "Mr. Dacron, I've just realized we're going to need someone to pilot the shuttlecraft to bring our officers here from the ships. I'd like you to be the chauffeur."

"Aye, sir," Dacron replied, scratching his shoulder. "May I take an oatmeal bath here on the station before leaving, sir?" Ricardo nodded, and Dacron went off in search of the locker room.

Ricardo followed Smirk and Crisco as they made their way toward the central area of the station. Their walking tour down the Promenade proved that the station more than lived up to Starfreak Command's off-the-record assessment: "a dump."

Raw sewage ran down a makeshift gutter next to the walkway. At one corner, wild dogs fought over the body of a dead rat. Bridgeoran gangs had defaced the walls with graffiti and defiantly toilet-papered the second-story railing.

About every third storefront had been vandalized by the departing Carcinogens or gutted by a Bridgeoran terrorist bomb. Stores that managed to remain in business catered to the few lowlife alien travelers who still patronized the station. There was a gun store, a combination pawnshop/sperm bank called Pawn 'N' Spawn, a Narcotics-R-Us outlet, and a shop with security bars on its doors and windows, plastered with signs stating "Checks cashed" and "We pay top $$$ for blood plasma."

The three officers paused at a section of the Promenade where adult video stores competed for customers: one advertised "rated XXX," the next said "rated XXXXX," and a third said "rated X^{10}."

"That reminds me," said Smirk. "I'm very interested in meeting your science officer."

"Lieutenant Jazzy Fax? I'm afraid she's away on a mission," Crisco replied. "She and Dr. Brassiere took a shuttle through the wormhole to get some takeout food. There's a great little Thai place in the Gummi Quadrant that's far superior to anything in this sector. Fax won't be back for a day or two."

"Mmmph," Smirk said. "In that case, can you direct me to Quirk's?"

"It's this way," Crisco said, escorting them farther down the corridor, "though I'd rather not spend much time there. I thought we'd have supper in my quarters before I show you to your special guest rooms."

Just ahead, two boys dangled their feet from the second-floor balcony. The captains recognized them from the personnel photos: it was Crisco's son, Joke, and Quirk's nephew, Eggnog. They were fooling with a phaser. Eggnog aimed it at random and fired, zapping an alien bystander. The boys shook with giggles. Eggnog cranked the phaser to a higher setting and took aim at another stranger.

"Aren't you going to stop them?" Ricardo asked, alarmed.

"There's no need," Crisco answered, checking his watch. "Security Chief Dodo should be coming along right about ... now." He glanced up from his watch. Sure enough, Dodo emerged from the shadows, grabbed each boy by an ear, and pulled the pair to their feet. "So we're being naughty again, are we?" Dodo sneered.

"Ouch!" Eggnog exclaimed. "You keep your hands off my private parts!"

As Crisco ushered the captains down the hallway, he explained, "They go through a variation on that scene every day at this time."

"You don't say," Smirk commented.

"That's nothing," Crisco went on. "When it comes to consistency, nobody beats the four P.M. Major Vera eruption. She's our station's version of Old Faithful." Just ahead of them, a crowd had gathered. "We're just in time," Crisco observed. "Excuse me, please."

Crisco left the two captains standing at the outskirts of the crowd and pushed his way through to the center. Major Vera stood there, and she was fuming.

"What's this I hear about an order from the federation limiting imports of tin?" she hollered at Crisco. "You know our Bridgeoran ear chains are made from tin. What do you expect us to do, roll over and play dead?"

"Major Vera," Crisco began, "it's just a temporary measure—"

"I don't care!" she screamed. "You federation types think you can just waltz in here and violate our Bridgeoran sovereignty! I've had it up to here with you people!" Smirk and Ricardo noticed that many in the crowd were mouthing Major Vera's words along with her, as if this were a play they'd seen enough times to memorize.

Major Vera went on, "We fought long and hard against the Carcinogens, and now it's our turn to decide the destiny of our people and our planet! Badger for Bridgeorans! Badger for Bridgeorans!" As the crowd listlessly took up the chant—"Badger for Bridgeorans . . . Badger for Bridgeorans"—Crisco quietly slipped out of their midst and returned to Smirk and Ricardo.

"Let's go," he urged. "From here on she starts getting weepy about the hardship and sacrifice of the Bridgeoran struggle. You don't want to hear her bawl right now. It'll spoil your appetite for supper."

"Gee, don't you ever get tired of going through these routines with the kids and Major Vera day after day?" Smirk inquired.

"Tired?" Crisco repeated blankly, as if the thought had never occurred to him.

Smirk didn't pursue the point, for they had arrived at the doorstep of Quirk's bar. "I'll catch you guys tomorrow," he announced. "I'm going to see about renting a suite with a classy hollowdame."

"Captain, I thought we'd have supper and a nice long chat—" Crisco began, but Smirk had already blended into the ragtag crowd around the bar.

Obviously peeved at the way Smirk took off, Crisco said, half to himself, "Okay, then, forget supper." Abruptly he turned on his heel and headed down the Promenade, barking over his shoulder to Ricardo, "I'll show you to your guest quarters." Ricardo stepped after him briskly, trying to keep up.

Soon afterward, Ricardo surveyed his room. Crisco had left him there after mumbling something about how the lack of closet space forced them to use this spot for storage. The windowless cell was stuffed with metal pails, mops, rags, and plastic signs reading "Caution—Wet Floor."

So these are our "special" accommodations, Ricardo thought. *This station is in even worse shape than I expected.* There wasn't a mattress or a cot to be found, so Ricardo created a makeshift bed from sponges and mop yarn. Lying down in the dark, he listened to the water dripping off the sweating pipes overhead and tried to sleep.

Late that night, Crisco made his final rounds before bedtime and stopped at Dodo's office.

"Everything all right?" Crisco inquired of Dodo, who surveyed the glowing panels of his security monitor.

"All except for one unidentified life form down in the

Ricardo created a makeshift bed from sponges and
mop yarn.

basement level," Dodo reported. "I'll have a security guard check it out. It's probably a vagrant looking for a place to sleep. You'd think they could find a better place than a janitor's closet."

Crisco glanced at the monitor and replied, "No need to check it out. That's Captain Ricardo in his 'guest quarters.'"

2

Send in
the Clowns

EVENING CAME, and morning followed: the second day.
Dacron piloted the shuttlecraft toward Geek Space
Nine with Mr. Smock and Cmdr. Wilson Piker as
passengers. Their captains had ordered Smock and Piker
to begin counseling the belligerent Major Vera Obese.

Sitting in his window seat, Smock closed his eyes and
began to psych himself up by droning the mantras he'd
acquired at various weekend retreats ("Ommmmm...
gummmmm...bummmmm"). He needed all the courage
he could muster to get past the first and most distasteful
step of this mission: having Piker fill him in on the details.

Both officers were to have received a briefing packet the
night before, but thanks to a bureaucratic mixup at Starfreak Headquarters, only one packet had been sent—to
Piker. That meant that Smock had to rely on Piker's ability
to read, understand and interpret a complex document.
The very thought of it made Smock's ears curl. The only
saving grace was that by soliciting Piker's help right at
this moment, Smock could get him to stop whistling "It's
a Small World."

Piker seemed flattered when Smock asked him for a
summary of Vera's condition. Setting aside the tabloid
newspaper he'd been reading, Piker stroked his beard in a
gesture that temporarily raised his IQ level half a point.

"Let's see," Piker said, "what *did* they say about her? I just read that stuff last night."

Smock prompted, "Our initial orders noted that the station's residents have little depth of personality. The report probably focused on one or two broad character traits."

"Yeah, that's right," Piker said. "Now I remember. Major Vera shows only two emotions. She's either mad or sad." He flashed a self-satisfied smile and flipped open the newspaper again, turning to a story headlined NUN FROM UFO GIVES BIRTH TO ELVIS-SHAPED RUTABAGA.

"Mr. Piker . . . " Smock said, hoping to catch him before he started whistling again.

Piker looked up from the newspaper. "Mmmm?"

"We will need more than that if we are to develop a coaching strategy," Smock said. "Did the briefing papers give any idea how to go about it?"

"I don't think so," Piker said. He screwed up his face in concentration for a minute, then continued, "No, they just said she has these two emotions. So maybe we should try to move her up a notch, to three emotions. Let's see— what new one should we work on? Right now she's either mad or sad. Hmmm, mad or sad . . . mad or sad . . . I know! Glad!"

This time, when Piker returned to his newspaper, Smock decided not to pursue the issue. Instead he sat and wondered how they could best avoid stirring up Major Vera's temper. Capt. Smirk had said that Vera was "difficult," and like most Vultures, Smock preferred to keep his distance from anyone who was likely to make a scene.

As Dacron maneuvered the craft into a parking space in the shuttlebay of the space station, the two officers rose and moved to the shuttlecraft's rear door. Dacron pressed a button, and the door swung open. Major Vera Obese stood in the shuttlebay waiting for them, fists clenched at her sides, her face obviously set in Emotion Number One.

Smock and Piker shrank back from the doorway. Piker

muttered, "Dacron, are you sure it's safe to get out?"

"This *has* been classified as a Class M station..." Dacron affirmed. The two officers tiptoed through the door toward Vera. "...with M standing for 'masochistic,'" Dacron added, then instantly shut the door behind them.

The remark prompted the two officers to turn back toward the safety of the shuttle, but Dacron was already taking off with a little screech that indicated the thrusters were low on air.

Cautiously they turned around again to face Major Vera. Out of the side of his mouth, Piker said to Smock, "Never mind—Dacron will pay for that. I booby-trapped the shuttle's fire sprinklers to drench him as soon as he turns off the engine."

Vera's stare bore down on them. "So you're the clowns who are supposed to bring me up to speed, huh?" she barked. "Well, I may have to put up with you, but I don't have to like it!"

Vera turned around and stomped out of the shuttlebay, muttering to herself. Smock and Piker followed, trying to avoid being left behind as she weaved through the unfamiliar corridors. Smock got close enough to hear her mumbling indignantly about dullimia.

"Major, that diagnosis was considered classified information," Smock remarked. "How did you hear about it?"

"I bought it from Quirk," Vera snapped. "He sold me the whole story for five bars of gold-pressed laudanum."

"Who is this 'Quirk'?" Smock inquired.

"You'll find out soon enough," Vera replied. "I'm taking you to his saloon." She added under her breath, "And losing you there, I hope."

They entered Quirk's. Vera took a corner barstool, Piker sat down next to her, and Smock sat on the other side of Piker, glad to have such a large, heavy object between him and Major Vera.

Quirk approached them. "Morning, folks," he said. "Care to try our breakfast buffet? All you can eat, only

$10.99, and now certified shape-shifter-free by the Star-freak Board of Health."

"We don't need breakfast, Quirk," Vera snarled. "Just pour three shots of Southern Cross Comfort." Turning to Smock and Piker, she asked, "And what do you two want?"

Neither of them had heard of the Bridgeoran liquor, but they were eager to fit in with local custom. "Uh, I'll have the same," Piker said. Smock nodded.

"Nine Southern Cross Comforts coming up," Quirk responded. As he lined up the shot glasses and poured, he said quietly to Vera, "Major, are you sure about this? You know that starship officers are used to drinking that replicated stuff. The genuine Southern Cross I serve could put them under the table."

"That's exactly what I have in mind, Quirk," Vera whispered fiercely, "to get them to forget about this 'coaching' baloney—for today, at least, and maybe longer if they work up a big enough hangover."

Vera picked up the first of her shot glasses and gestured toward Piker and Smock. "Our traditional toast is *Niks-glacht vwien scheinkz*. That's Old Bridgeoran for 'Screw the Carcinogens,' " she told them.

The other two raised their glasses, and Vera downed her liquor in a single gulp. Piker and Smock did the same.

Piker set down his glass on the bar. "Say, that's one smooth drink," he observed.

"Remarkably so," said Smock, unable to keep the surprise out of his voice. He'd expected Vera to ambush them with firewater.

"Have another," Vera urged, a hint of a smile playing on her lips. Piker was turned toward Vera, so he didn't notice that Smock's eyebrows were already beginning to melt as the Southern Cross entered his system.

After Piker swallowed his second shot, he said, "Speaking of Old Bridgeoran, I was wondering how come you people call yourselves Bridgeorans when the name of your planet is Badger. Why don't you call yourselves Badgers?"

"We don't need breakfast, Quirk," Vera snarled.

"Perhaps to avoid being confused with the Big Ten football team of the same name," Smock said, clearly eager to placate Vera; but she waved off his disclaimer, looking more relaxed than she had since they'd met.

"We're called Bridgeorans because of this series of ridges on the bridge of the nose," she said. "Bridge . . . ridges . . . Bridgeorans. Get it?"

"Gottit," Piker slurred. "That sakes a lot of mense." He seemed to be having trouble synchronizing the movement of his upper lip with his lower lip.

Smock sipped his third glassful, oblivious of the steam rising from the edges of his collar.

"Yeah, that's interesting," Piker continued with exaggerated care, as if pronouncing each syllable took as much concentration as threading a needle. "Bridgeorans from Badger. It's kinda like the name for people from Alaska, my home state. They're called Alaskans." Vera waited for Piker to finish his point, but apparently he thought he already had.

Vera gestured at Quirk; he cleared off the empty shot glasses and set refills before them. "So you're from Alaska, huh?" Vera prompted. "What city?"

"Valdez," Piker said, adding proudly, "I've made the place famous. People hear 'Valdez' and think of me."

"Huh. When I hear 'Valdez,' " Vera countered, "I think of the big oil-tanker spill in the late twentieth century."

"Well, okay," Piker allowed, "maybe that's more famous right now. But someday people are going to realize that I've had a much bigger impact on the galaxy than that oil spill."

"An apt comparison," Smock mused. He stared upward as if trying to focus on the mother-in-law-tongue plant in a hanging pot overhead.

"Ah, Valdez, Valdez," Piker went on. "Lotsa good memories of growing up there. And some not-so-good memories, too. Like the day my mom abonded . . . ababbed . . ."

he waggled his jaw between his fingers and finally got it out: *"abandoned* us."

"You grew up in a single-parent family, then?" Vera asked. Warmed by the drinks, she seemed to be mellowing toward Piker.

Piker nodded. "The worst part was when my dad took over the cooking. Have you ever had moose meat warmed in a microwave oven?" Vera shook her head. "It tastes like leather," Piker complained. He tossed back another shot and added, "Then again, it tastes like leather no matter how you cook it."

"Sounds like a rough life," Vera said, leaning on her elbows and gazing intently at Piker.

Quirk, noticing that Smock was drooping, came around to the patrons' side of the bar and fastened the seat belt of the barstool around Smock's midriff.

"I had a hard childhood too," Vera confessed to Piker. Obviously struggling to keep her voice even, she said, "The Carcinogen occupation—well, they did everything they could to break us. You can't imagine the cruelty."

"I can jusht imagine," Piker commiserated, pronouncing the words with great care, "how un ... im ... ag ... in ... able the cruelty was."

"It's toughened me up," Vera said. "But sometimes I can't help feel that my heart is being ripped out."

The sob in Vera's voice penetrated the fog around Smock, and he sensed that Vera could break out in a maelstrom of emotion any minute. He began fumbling with the buckle of the seat belt and looking around blearily for an exit.

"The worst times are when I see an injustice done to a fellow Bridgeoran," Vera went on, her face a mask of maudlinity, "like when our spiritual leader, the ChiroPractor, was killed." Her voice caught; she sobbed once, then went on. "Or when the government wanted to build a freeway on one of our moons, so they tossed this old farmer and his servants Buffy and Jody off their land." She drew a breath shakily, with the sobs just beneath the surface making a *wuh-wuh-wuh* sound.

Piker became uneasy as Vera turned more mawkish. He tried to think of how Counselor Troit would comfort someone who was feeling this way. Finally he offered, "It must be very hard for you."

"Oh, it is, it is!" Vera shrieked—and like a thunderstorm finally letting loose, she began bawling voraciously.

Quirk set a jumbo box of Kleenex tissues on the counter in front of her and walked away, muttering, "Bad for business, bad for business."

We've got to stop her somehow, Piker thought, *before she gets hysterical*. After a glance at Smock revealed that the Vulture was still fumbling with the seat belt clasp, Piker realized that it was up to him to engineer a peaceful conclusion to this volatile episode.

Vera blew her nose with a resounding *honnnnnk*, then said in a wobbly voice, "Everybody thinks I'm so hard. Actually I'm tough and leathery on the outside but soft and mushy on the inside, like a bad orange that you get in your lunchbox. I'm so tired of fighting, of always having to be the strong one . . . *yadda yadda yadda . . .*"

"*Yadda yadda yadda. . . .*" The input to Piker's brain underwent a dimensional shift. His male listening gland—impeded by the alcohol in his blood—had finally kicked in, buffering him from Vera's tirade. "*Yadda yadda yadda . . .*"

Undistracted by the content of Vera's message, Piker could finally concentrate on his own thoughts, such as they were. He remembered something that seemed related to Vera's problem. *Maybe it will help cheer her up. Yeah, it could take her from mad to sad to . . . glad!*

When Vera paused to rub her eyes with a tissue, Piker interjected, "Your story reminds me of an old crewmate, Yasha Tar. She had a hard childhood, too."

"Really?" Vera asked. She pulled out an oversized handkerchief and began mopping up the puddle of tears on the bar.

"Maybe even worse than yours," Piker said cheerfully. "She said she used to run and hide from the grape gangs."

"Gee," Vera said, "it would mean so much to me to talk to another woman in the same boat." She brightened. Smock looked over at her cautiously, and Piker began to relax. Vera speculated, "Maybe she could tell me how she triumphed over her difficult past."

"That may indeed prove very helpful," Smock observed, giving up on the seat belt and reaching for a handful of salted peanuts.

"I'd love to meet this Yasha Tar," Vera told Piker. "How can I get in touch with her?"

"You can't," Piker replied. "She's dead."

Vera stared at Piker in disbelief for a moment. Then understanding dawned, and she drew a deep breath and wailed at the top of her lungs. Finally, rage broke through her tears.

"You idiot!" she screamed. "You have been *no* help at *all*!"

Vera reached overhead, yanked the potted plant from its mooring, and smashed it over Piker's head with a booming *thunk*. She stormed out of the bar, wailing.

Smock brushed the potting soil off his shoulder and told his dazed companion, "Congratulations, Mr. Piker. You managed to engage her mad and sad facets simultaneously."

Dodo sat back in the chair with his feet up on his Security office desk. "How do you do, Mr. Wart," Dodo rasped. "So nice to have you on our station."

In reply, Wart merely grunted. He knew sarcasm when he heard it, and Dodo's gravelly voice fairly hummed with it.

"You'll enjoy working my Security detail," Dodo said. "There's a real need for law-and-order personnel here on

Dodo sat back in the chair with his feet up on his
Security office desk.

the station, unlike the tranquil atmosphere of, say, a starship."

Wart emitted a low growl. After several seconds of clenching and unclenching his fists, he managed to rumble, "I am not here to work on your staff. We should begin your training session."

"To see if you can cure my dullimia, you mean?"

Wart's eyes shifted uneasily, but he maintained, "My orders say only that I am to give you career counseling."

"I know Starfreak is calling it dullimia and sending your crews here to 'cure' us. Nothing on this station gets by me," Dodo boasted. "In this particular case, I had to buy the information from someone. But at only seven bars of gold-pressed laudanum, I figure I made a pretty good deal."

"Whether or not you think you need the training," Wart countered, "I have my orders."

"Don't be ridiculous," Dodo said. "It's impossible for me to have dullimia. I'm a shape-shifter. I've twisted myself into more dimensions than you can count, Kringle."

"You are confusing form with substance," Wart told him, "though even your form is unimpressive." Dodo bristled, but Wart continued, "Your present human manifestation leaves much to be desired. You look like a crayon left out in the sun too long."

"I could perfect the details if I wanted to," Dodo claimed haughtily. "I'm just too busy."

Wart scoffed.

"Don't push me, Kringle," Dodo warned. "I could deport you from this station so fast it would make your ponytail spin. After all, you do come from a criminal background."

"What do you mean?" Wart demanded.

"Don't be coy," Dodo said. "Everybody knows the story: that you're Wart, son of Moe, whose treachery led to the massacre of the Kringles at Kittylitter."

It took only a half-second for Wart to leap forward and wrap his hands around Dodo's neck. In the next half-second, Dodo shape-shifted in a defensive maneuver that turned him into a Kringle.

"You wouldn't strangle a fellow Kringle, would you?" Dodo reasoned. "Code of honor and all that?"

Wart grunted in disgust and loosened his grip. He studied Dodo's Kringle manifestation and judged, "You have the forehead all wrong. Observe mine: it is like Jell-O Chocolate Pudding swirled with a spoon."

"I'll work on it," Dodo promised, rubbing the raw grip marks Wart had left around his neck.

"Did you notice whether there's an ice machine down the hall?" came Piker's voice in the dark of the guest quarters.

Smock and Wart shifted impatiently in their cots. Every time they began drifting off to sleep, Piker would start jabbering again. Smock told him, "Our guest bathroom has a faucet and a dispenser of disposable cups, Mr. Piker."

"I don't want a drink. I want ice," Piker said. "I need to hold it against this lump on my head. That potted plant Major Vera dropped on me was heavy."

"There is no ice available," Wart told him. "Go to sleep!"

Around midnight, Piker finally shut up for good, and the three slept. Wart's snoring resonated through their guest room. It was so loud that they didn't have a chance to hear the insidious tear in the fabric of space. The opening appeared next to their chain-pull toilet. The three officers were still fast asleep as they plunged into the void.

3

Doctors'
Disorders

EVENING CAME, and morning followed: the third day.
Capt. Ricardo carefully brought the glass of orange
juice to his lips, holding his head rigid to avoid stirring up the zinging pain in his neck. Two nights of sleeping
on a pile of damp cleaning equipment had aggravated his
chronic neuralgia. Now he was having breakfast at Quirk's
before his appointment with one of the station's back-alley
chiropractors.

Capt. Smirk sat down next to him. "Say, Jean-Lucy,"
Smirk began, "do you know whether Lieutenant Fax has
come back from the wormhole? She's not in her quarters,
and the station's personnel locator isn't working."

"No, I haven't seen her," Ricardo said. "I've been looking
for Commander Piker myself. He hasn't yet reported to
me on the first counseling session he and Mr. Smock were
supposed to conduct with Major Vera."

"Funny," Smirk mused, "I haven't seen Smock, either.
He's usually up by 0430 hours doing his fifty pushups and
one-hundred situps. Oh, well," Smirk said, shaking his
head, "never mind. I've got to find this Lieutenant Fox—
er, Fax." He laughed and added, "Freudian slip. She *is* a
fox, isn't she?" Smirk jumped up and strode energetically
out the door, a man on a mission.

Ricardo gazed wistfully after him, a little envious of

Smirk's romantic zeal. Ricardo himself rarely took time out for affairs of the heart, although he did have a girlfriend of sorts, a rogue archeologist named Stosh. Stosh visited his ship when she could find time between digs, and on these rare occasions she and Ricardo usually managed to create a few sparks by rubbing their artifacts together.

Ricardo picked up his toasted English muffin. Trying to keep his aching neck straight, he reached awkwardly for the bowl that held serving packets of jelly. *Oh, well*, he told himself, *it's just as well Stosh isn't here now. I'm so stiff I could barely bend over to kiss the Rosetta Stone.*

"You expect me to give you a rundown on Dr. Brassiere?" groused Dr. Lynyrd "Moans" McCaw. "For Pete's sake, I'm a doctor, not a physician referral service."

Dr. Beverage Flusher folded her arms across her chest and sat back in her passenger seat. The shuttlecraft was zipping them toward Geek Space Nine. "Fine," she replied. "But if you don't tell me what's wrong with him, you're going to have to coach him all by yourself. It's not my fault that Starfreak never sent me my copy of the briefing." She fastened her seat belt with an emphatic *click*.

"Oh, all right," McCaw said, grasping the armrest to steady himself as the shuttle bounced up and down. "Hey, android," he called up to the front, "can't you steer around this turbulence?"

"I am sorry, Doctor," Dacron said from the driver's seat, "but the proximity of the wormhole seems to be creating a wind shear effect. Please observe that as the captain of this vessel I have now turned on the 'fasten seat belts' sign."

McCaw turned back to Flusher and said, "The main thing about this Dr. Julio Brassiere is that he thinks he's really hot stuff, just because he finished Starfreak Academy Medical School in only six weeks and paid off his tuition by rewriting some of the textbooks. Lots of meaningless flash and dazzle, if you ask me."

"I have now turned on the 'fasten seat belts' sign."

Flusher nodded, trying to concentrate on what McCaw was saying, although the turbulence was making her stomach do flip-flops.

"Meanwhile," McCaw said, "he's neglecting the really important parts of his medical career. Heck, his golf game is laughable. Would you believe he's got a handicap of thirty-four?"

Flusher held a hand to her mouth and belched daintily, trying to relieve her inner turbulence. "Did the report say anything else?" Flusher asked. "What about his social life?" She noticed that her hands were trembling, and she guessed that her face was turning pale.

"Just a minute," McCaw said. Again he leaned toward the front of the craft and called up to Dacron. "Hey, android, do we get any snacks on this flight?"

"They are in the wall compartment labeled 'munchies,' " Dacron replied, grasping the edge of his control console as the craft dipped and bounced.

McCaw opened the wall compartment and, after sorting through the snacks, settled on a package of beef jerky sticks. "Brassiere's social life is a bust," McCaw told Flusher. "He goes jumping around like a dog that got loose from its chain, all wide-eyed and yappy, but nobody will give him the time of day. He reminds me a lot of your kid—what's his name? Westy? Woosy?"

"Westerly," Flusher replied through clenched teeth. She could feel herself beginning to sweat; that meant she had passed the point of no return.

McCaw bit off the end of a beef jerky stick and, between chews, said to Flusher, "I figure Brassiere is one of those ivory-tower types—full of textbook knowledge but useless under fire."

The smell of McCaw's beef jerky wafted over Flusher in waves, breaking down her last reserves of control. Gasping "excuse me," she grabbed at the seatback pouch in front of her and located a spacesickness bag in the nick of time.

Oblivious of Flusher's retching, McCaw stared up at the

ceiling, twiddled his beef jerky stick, and mused, "His dossier said Brassiere is all hepped up about practicing 'frontier medicine.' Ha! I bet he wouldn't know a sick person if they keeled over right in front of him."

Flusher glared at him, wiping the sweat off her forehead. She neatly folded down the top of the bulging spacesickness bag. As she got up to use the shuttlecraft's washroom, she handed the bag to McCaw.

"What's this?" he asked.

"Dessert," she told him, and tottered down the aisle.

McCaw opened the bag, sniffed its contents, then held it at arm's length. "Good gawd!" he exclaimed. "Just when I thought airline food couldn't possibly get any worse . . . !"

A few minutes later, the two doctors were wandering down the Promenade of the space station. No one had met their shuttlecraft, so they hoped to find their own way to Sick Bay.

Noticing many Ferengi among those in the Promenade, McCaw remarked, "Looks like I went into the wrong business. An orthodontist could make a fortune here."

Flusher saw someone striding toward them from a side corridor. "Is that Dr. Brassiere?" she asked.

McCaw grimaced. "That's him."

"You must be Dr. Flusher and Dr. McCaw," Brassiere began, approaching them with his hand extended. "I'm Dr. Julio Brassiere." He clasped Flusher's palm, then vigorously pumped McCaw's hand. "Welcome to Geek Space Nine. What do you think of it so far?"

Flusher replied, "It's quite—"

"Wonderful place, isn't it?" Brassiere interrupted. "So new and challenging, and best of all, we've got enough casualties to make the day go by quickly. Let's get to Sick Bay. I'll give you the *grahnd* tour." He ushered them down the corridor.

McCaw began, "We need to—"

"So sorry I couldn't meet your shuttlecraft," Brassiere butted in, "but I was just finishing a gill transplant on a

Guppyan freighter captain who came down with a bad case of ick after docking here. More precisely, the operation was a combination gill/gall bladder transplant, the first in the galaxy. It'll make quite a writeup for the *Nude English Journal of Medicine*, if I do say so myself."

Flusher commented, "My, that's quite—"

"Say, do you two ever go out together socially? Maybe you'd like to come on a double date tonight with myself and Lieutenant Jazzy Fax." Brassiere blithely carried on, failing to notice that his companions recoiled in horror at the thought of socializing with each other. "That is, if I can get her to agree to come with me," Brassiere said. "She's turned down all my offers so far, but you know what they say: three-hundred-and-thirty-third time's the charm."

They rounded a corner, and Brassiere stopped. "By the way," he said, "before we go any further, I'll save you lots of trouble by making it clear that I don't need any treatment for dullimia."

McCaw said, "How did you—"

"I have my sources," Brassiere said, attempting a worldly smile that looked out of place on his choirboy features. "I drove a hard bargain for this information, too. It only cost me fifty-three bars of gold-pressed laudanum."

Flusher said, "We still have to—"

"I'm afraid I must insist," Brassiere said. "I can prove to you that I'm not infected by dullimia. I'll do a reprise of a persona I took on recently when I was possessed by the spirit of an alien criminal. That'll show you how much depth I have. You'll hardly believe I'm the same person."

He stepped back into a doorway, away from the pedestrian traffic. Flusher and McCaw watched uneasily.

Brassiere began his schtick by breathing heavily to work up a head start on the characterization. He assumed a facial expression almost as fierce as a Cub Scout's imitation of the big bad wolf.

Dr. McCaw rolled his eyes heavenward. He hated watch-

ing someone make a fool of himself by trying—and failing—to practice Method medicine.

Finally Brassiere lowered his voice and intoned, "Give
me what I want, or the doctor dies," managing to sound
about as menacing as the Jolly Green Giant.

Flusher started looking nauseous again, and McCaw
blurted out, "Holy mother of pearl, man, you're even worse
off than they said you were."

"Hey, Georgie, old pal, how are you?" Smiles O'Brine gave
Georgie LaForgery a bear hug.

"Long time no see, Smiles," Georgie responded. "You
remember Mr. Snot, don't you? I'm sure you've met him
sometime when he's been aboard our *Endocrine*. Mr. Snot,
this is Smiles O'Brine. He used to be the UltraFax Chief
on our ship."

"How d'ye do?" came the polite response from Montgomery Ward Snot, Capt. Smirk's chief engineer. "Nice
station ye have here." Then he dropped the pleasantries
and assumed a serious expression. "Where's the bar?"

"I'll take ya there," Smiles offered. As they walked down
the corridor to Quirk's, Smiles shook his head, grinned at
Georgie, and said, "It's sure good to see a familiar face
from the ship after looking at the parade of freaks around
here these past few months. And of course there hasn't
been a single engineer among them to trade some shop
talk with me. How are things in Engineering on the *Endocrine*, anyway?"

"They're fine," Georgie said. "In fact, Captain Ricardo
just approved my department's budget. We've allocated
money for kneepads that people can use when crawling
around in the Jiffy Tubes."

"Great," Smiles responded. "It's about time. Even before
I left, people were crawling around in those tubes about
once a day."

Georgie nodded. "The emergencies haven't let up," he
said. "The Jiffy Tubes aren't just a quick-and-dirty alter-

native to the Crewmover anymore. They've become a standard bypass route."

The three officers stepped up to Quirk's bar and placed their orders, then sought out a corner table. Smiles told Georgie, "I'm glad you could come to our station, even if it did take this coaching malarkey to bring you here."

"Hey, Smiles," Georgie said, holding up his hands as if to disclaim any part of the idea, "I don't buy into that stuff for a minute. I'm just following orders."

Their drinks arrived. "I'm glad to hear you say that," Smiles said, lifting his mug of ale. "When I paid ten bars of gold-pressed laudanum only to hear that you'd come because we've supposedly got dullimia—well, let me tell you, I decided I'd fight any man with the guts to say that to my face."

"Gentlemen, let's be reasonable, so we can get down t' some serrrious carousin'," Snot said. "Just between us, we'll forget all about this coachin' idea. After all, what does an engineer need a personality for, anyway?" He raised his glass. "Here's mud in your eye."

"Here, here," Georgie and Smiles echoed, and the three of them clinked their glasses together.

Behind the bar, Chief Bartender Quirk was deeply engrossed in a phone conversation about a hot tip he'd provided someone—that it was Ricardo's crew, not Smirk's, in the nursing home. "Yes, I got the money you wired me," Quirk said. "But I thought you were going to throw in some Green Stamps, too.

" . . . You're darn right that was a good tip. . . . How did I find out? Easy, my friend. All my Hollowsweets are bugged, and Crisco talks in his sleep. . . . I agree—he doesn't seem like the Hollowsweets type, but you wouldn't believe the kinky programs he asks for.

"Hey, I've gotta go. Guano just walked in. She's my so-called mentor from the Ten-Foreplay lounge on Captain Ricardo's ship. At least I think that's her; they said to expect somebody in a ridiculous hat."

Within half an hour, Quirk had somehow persuaded Guano to serve as his apprentice barmaid. After instructing her in his hard-sell techniques for the bar's high-markup specialty drinks, he asked, "Any questions?"

"Just one," Guano said, clutching her apron. "Who's that scary-looking alien sitting at the end of the bar?"

Quirk followed her gaze to a gorilla-like creature with a bald, mottled scalp, stern eyebrows, and a deep frown that shaded into a gargantuan drooping chin—sort of an aged Chewbacca.

"Oh, the Leerian. He's a regular," Quirk said. "He's here whenever we're open, always with a beer in his hand. I don't know much about him, except that every day when he comes in, all my other customers yell 'Norm!' "

Guano studied the Leerian and nodded.

"If you're interested in the locals," Quirk went on, "I could fix you up with Dodo, our security chief. He's just your type—no eyebrows."

Something caught Guano's attention. "Look. There's Captain Ricardo," she said. "Let me see if I can sell him a specialty drink."

"Go get 'em, barmaid," Quirk urged.

"Good afternoon, Captain," Guano said, sashaying up to Ricardo as he entered the room. "Welcome to Quirk's. Would you care for a Hubble Smoothie? It's the only drink that comes with a guarantee: two swallows and you won't be able to focus on anything."

"No, Guano," said Ricardo. "I've only stopped in here again to see if Commander Piker has turned up. He hasn't been seen anywhere in the station today. Do you know where he is?"

"Do I know where he is?" Guano repeated, stalling for time. She held a hand to her forehead and muttered, "A question on the whereabouts of a patron. This is one of those policy issues that Quirk covered in his orientation. . . ."

Guano glanced toward Quirk and saw that he was

mouthing something. She peered at him. He mouthed it several more times, exaggerating so she could read his lips. Finally Guano understood the correct response, turned toward Ricardo, and stated, "He's not here."

Ricardo turned and left.

"That was a close one," remarked Lt. Jazzy Fax, who had been sitting at the bar eavesdropping on Guano's conversation with Ricardo. "You wouldn't want to violate the solemn oath of confidentiality between a bartender and his customer." Fax smiled her Mona Lisa smile, took a sip of her tea, and struck a demure pose.

Guano quickly sized up Jazzy Fax as the bar's resident Zen figure, with her bemused know-it-all smile, calm demeanor, and weird, mysterious past. Guano knew this through the scientific principle "It takes one to know one."

Guano had already heard that Fax was a symbiont whose old sluglike inner creature had previously inhabited a brusque adventurer, Kermit Fax. That would explain the cosmopolitan look about Jazzy that seemed to say: *I've been around the galaxy more than once. Go ahead, try and impress me. Just try.* The air around her fairly shimmered with inaccessibility vibes.

As if summoned by a whistle audible only to the chronically masochistic, Dr. Julio Brassiere chose that moment to bring his drink over to the barstool next to her. "Hello, Jazzy," he said, flashing a dazzling smile.

"Julio." Fax nodded at him, smiled for a microsecond, then studied her teacup. "The answer is no."

Brassiere looked crushed. "What do you mean? I haven't asked you anything yet."

"Every day about this time you hit on me to have dinner with you," Fax said. "I thought I'd save you the trouble."

"As a *mah*tter of fact, I had something else to say, too, besides asking you to have dinner with me," Brassiere whined with the poignancy of a cocker spaniel who'd just lost his bone. "I wanted to share with you a very important medical advancement that I made today."

"Oh? What's that?" Fax cocked her eyebrow, almost curious.

"I performed a vasectomy on myself, and I was hoping you'd help me test-drive it." Brassiere showed off his profile, smiled another hotshot surgeon's smile, and took a gulp of his drink. But his smile faded when he turned back to check Fax's response to his come-on. Fax was staring straight ahead, her face blank.

"Jazzy? Jazzy?" Brassiere prompted. He snapped his fingers in front of her nose, and she came to her senses with a start.

"Oooh," said Fax. "I fell asleep with my eyes open again. That's been happening a lot lately. Now, where were we?"

Brassiere pouted. "I'd just given you what I hoped would be an irresistible invitation."

"Oh, yes. Now I know where we are," Fax said. She smoothed a wisp of hair back into her ponytail and purred, "I'm sorry, Julio. You're cute, but you're just not my type."

"You and I never seem to get beyond this stage," Brassiere said, sighing deeply. "Maybe we *do* have a touch of dullimia. Tell me, Jazzy, what is your type, anyway?"

She stared into the distance. "Someone seasoned, sophisticated and suave," she mused, smiling at a mental picture of her dreamboat. "Someone who can make me feel young and fresh and innocent. I may be old, Julio— in fact, my inner slug celebrates its three-hundredth birthday next Thursday—but just once I'd like to hear a come-on line I haven't yet heard or delivered in one of my many host bodies."

As Fax continued gazing off at nothing, the hairs on the back of her gazelle-like neck stood up. It was an effect often produced when Capt. Smirk walked up to a beautiful stranger and hovered a few inches behind her, as he was doing to Fax at this moment. "At last," Smirk said, "the woman who has haunted my dreams is here before me."

Dr. Brassiere glared at Smirk, then said to Fax, "Jazzy,

is this guy bothering you? I could wave around a big hypodermic needle to scare him off."

"Shhhh, Julio," Fax whispered. She seemed caught up in the mystery of Smirk's approach, choosing not to turn around and face him just yet. "I have the feeling a richly dramatic episode is about to occur," she added. "It's ... it's ... " she struggled to convey her profound emotions, " ... it's like being in the middle of a perfume commercial."

Fax's expectations were not disappointed. Capt. Smirk gently traced his fingertips over the leopard spots along her hairline. She closed her eyes, surrendering to the moment, obviously expecting an epiphany.

Smirk obliged, delivering the come-on of her dreams. "What a fanciful set of freckles you've got," Smirk murmured, "running from your forehead to your neck, and from there to—who knows?" His fingers hovered enticingly over Fax's neckline. "Why don't we play a round of 'Connect the Dots'?"

"Ooof!" "Woah!" "For th' love o'—" "Hey!" "What the—"

McCaw and Flusher and Snot and Georgie and Guano felt themselves yanked out of bed in their guest quarters and sucked into a yawning hole in the wall. As before, the fabric of space had torn neatly in the prescribed Home Ec manner, parallel to its selvage. As soon as the five crewmembers had tumbled inside, the hole closed again, trapping them there with Smock, Piker and Wart.

4

Here Comes
the Bribe

EVENING CAME, and morning followed: the fourth day. Capt. Smirk paced back and forth in Dodo's office. *"Now* how long has Gogetter had us on hold?" he demanded.

Capt. Ricardo consulted the clock on the office wall. "Twenty-five minutes," he replied.

Smirk fumed, "These people at headquarters think we've got nothing better to do than wait for their orders. For crying out loud, we're on an important mission here."

"What activities have you scheduled this morning?" Ricardo inquired mildly.

"I was hoping to meet Jazzy Fax in the beauty shop," Smirk said, "to watch her get her legs waxed. But she'll probably be done before Admiral Gogetter even comes back on the line." Smirk widened his pacing into a circle and picked up speed. Rounding a far corner, he nearly stumbled over a silver pail. He picked it up and peered inside. "What's this?"

"That must be Dodo's resting pail," Ricardo speculated. The two captains were calling Gogetter from Security Chief Dodo's office because most of the other Viewscreens on the station were out of order.

Ricardo added, "You know that Dodo reverts to his original gelatin form twice a day, don't you?" Smirk shook his head, and Ricardo said, "Oh, that's right. You never got a briefing packet.

"Well, the briefing said that Dodo uses up lots of energy when he shape-shifts into various forms," Ricardo went on, "so he recuperates by melting down into a glob. The briefing packet included a photograph of Dodo at rest. He looked rather like hasty pudding."

Smirk studied the pail again. "So he sleeps in here, huh? That explains the little mattress," he said, poking a cushion at the bottom of the pail. One corner of the cushion had a silk sash: "Shifty Posturepedic." There was also a paper label: "Warning! Do not remove this tag under penalty of law."

The Viewscreen crackled to life. "Hey, captains, how's the frontier shakin'?" Admiral Gogetter greeted them. Smirk joined Ricardo in front of the Viewscreen as Gogetter launched into his monologue.

"Last night I was proposing to my girlfriend Macy," Gogetter said, "when it occurred to me that you guys could use a little more incentive to finish this mission." He pulled out a can of shaving gel, spritzed the gel into his palm, spread it over his face, and began shaving with a double-edged razor.

"So as soon as I gave Macy the ring, I started making this list of perks. Mindy!" he called, and his second secretary appeared at once. "Fax this list to them, will you?" Gogetter turned to the Viewscreen and asked, "What's your fax number there, captains?" Smirk checked Dodo's fax machine and read the number aloud.

As Gogetter handed Mindy the list, he noticed a metal can of varnish remover sitting at the edge of his desk. "That reminds me..." he muttered. He cleared papers away from a spot on the desk, poured a glob of remover onto it, and started scraping off the varnish with a metal tool.

Gogetter's first secretary, Mandy, appeared at the office door escorting a man in a white short-sleeved shirt. "Doctor Yank is ready for your procedure, Admiral," Mandy said.

"Oh, yeah. The root canal," Admiral Gogetter said. "Come on in, Doc." Apparently, this was not the dentist's first house call; with practiced ease, he opened his carrying case and began setting up a portable dental workstation.

Paper emerged from Dodo's fax machine. "See what you think of those perks," Gogetter told Smirk and Ricardo. After making another swipe with the paint tool, he flicked a glob of varnish and remover into the wastebasket.

"If you finish your mission soon and do a decent job of it, you could earn some or all of those goodies," Gogetter added. With one hand he spritzed out more shaving cream; with the other, he poured varnish remover onto the desk.

Turning to the Viewscreen, Gogetter concluded, "Jim—Jean-Lucy—I'm counting on ya, guys." He dipped his hand into a pile of liquid and unwittingly spread varnish remover on the unshaved side of his face. "Geez, this stuff really stinks," he complained. "Mindy, next time get the unscented shave cream instead of the menthol kind."

Dr. Yank hovered at Gogetter's side, tools in hand. "Open wide," Dr. Yank said.

Their Viewscreen went blank, and Ricardo and Smirk turned to read Gogetter's list of perks:

money / supplies / missions to the hot and happening planets of your choice / extra vacation time / a "casual dress day" every Friday / coffee cake in all refreshment areas / reserved parking spots at Starfreak Headquarters in Milwaukee / subscriptions to *Chutney Reader* / golf outings for senior officers / new computer programs for your HolidayDecks / financial sponsorship of starship bowling teams

"Sounds terrific!" Smirk exclaimed, and Ricardo nodded his approval. "Let's debrief our crewmembers who've gotten here so far," Smirk added, "and see how their coaching sessions are coming along."

* * *

The captains' desire for an update on the coaching sessions was soon frustrated. They tried to count noses but found nary a nostril in sight.

A call to Dacron on Ricardo's *Endocrine* confirmed that he had shuttled eight crewmembers from their ships to the station on schedule. Yet according to the space station's temperamental personnel sensors—which were in working order for a full hour that morning—none of these crewmembers were present. In addition, neither captain could recall encountering the missing personnel for quite a while. Immediately they went to Crisco's office to complain.

Within minutes of their arrival, Crisco had made up his mind to solve the mysterious disappearance of Smirk's and Ricardo's crewmembers. More precisely, the captains made up Crisco's mind for him, threatening to squeal to Starfreak Command if the missing crewmembers didn't reappear soon. Crisco realized that if his bosses heard that people were disappearing from the station, they'd see him as truly incompetent, definitely a step down from their current view of him as just mildly inept.

"I don't understand it," Crisco thought out loud. "We hardly ever actually lose someone here. An occasional bombing casualty, maybe, but even then there are usually a few body parts left to identify."

Noticing that Ricardo and Smirk were glaring at him, Crisco stopped speculating and straightened his shoulders, all business. "We'll get to the bottom of this," he told the captains.

"You bet you will," Smirk told him. "I want my people back, on the double, so they can finish this coaching. Then we're off on our next mission. Gogetter promised us our pick of venues, so I'm taking my ship to the Planet of the Amazon Women."

"Keep us posted, Commander," Ricardo told Crisco. He, too, already had plans to claim his first perk—time off. His girlfriend Stosh had recently sent a postcard from her

latest archeological dig, and Ricardo intended to join her
at the site of this exciting new find. She'd just uncovered
the handlebars of a 1993 90th-anniversary model Harley-
Davidson.

The shuttlecraft zigged and zagged as it sped from the
starship parking area toward the space station; Dacron's
physical condition made it impossible for him to steer
straight. This was his first experience with Bus Driver's
Migraine, commonly induced by youthful passengers
screaming, fighting, bouncing in the seats, playing loud
music, throwing things, running up and down the aisles,
and making rude gestures out the window. Such was the
pandemonium on this particular leg of his route.

The shuttle was carrying only two passengers: Dr. Flusher's son, Westerly, and Wart's son, Smartalecsander. And
since Westerly was sitting quietly with his hands folded in
his lap, Dacron concluded that all the commotion was
coming from Smartalecsander.

Dacron tolerated the misbehavior for a few more minutes, but when a paper airplane sailed toward the front
and executed a 90-degree turn to lodge in Dacron's mock
ear canal, he decided he'd had enough. He slammed on
the shuttlecraft's brakes, pulled the airplane out of his ear,
and turned to face the offender.

"That is improper behavior, Smartalecsander," he ad-
monished. "My contract does not require me to tolerate
this treatment. I could take this shuttlecraft back to the
ship and turn you over to your school principal. Is that
what you want?"

"No," Smartalecsander said.

"Then I suggest you behave," Dacron concluded.

Smartalecsander caused no more trouble after that,
mostly because Dacron backed up the warning by confining
him with a straitjacket and tying him to a flight attendant's
jumpseat.

The young counterparts of Smartalecsander and Westerly were waiting to meet them when the shuttlecraft docked at Geek Space Nine. Cmdr. Crisco's son, Joke, and Quirk's nephew, Eggnog, had cut classes that morning as usual.

Joke was no longer the dweeb he'd been upon arriving at Geek Space Nine with his father. Several months of hanging around with his juvenile delinquent friend, Eggnog, had changed that. Theirs was the meanest gang on the station. And thanks to Eggnog's Ferengi instincts, it was the most profitable gang, too. Joke and Eggnog charged premium rates to forge parents' excuse notes letting kids skip school. They also took in protection money from all the other youngsters' lemonade stands.

Westerly and Smartalecsander left the shuttle and walked over to the other two. "Hi, you guys!" Westerly said. After one look at Westerly's flood pants and shirt pocket protector, Joke and Eggnog dismissed him with a curl of the lip.

Eggnog turned his best junior-grade-Ferengi sneer on Smartalecsander. "So you're the Kringle kid," Eggnog said. "Your Kringle forehead looks like a road kill."

"You should talk about foreheads," Smartalecsander shot back at the young Ferengi. "Who circumcised yours? Better sue him for malpractice." Smartalecsander cackled with laughter, and even Joke couldn't keep from giggling at the insult to his friend, though he stifled his laughter after Eggnog gave him a dirty look.

"Hey, guys," Westerly interjected, "let's try to get along, okay?"

"Shut up," Eggnog told him.

"Yeah, butt out," Smartalecsander said.

"Maybe we can use you, Kringle," Eggnog said to Smartalecsander. "You ever hot-wire a personal circuit for long distance calls?"

"Are you kidding? Every day," Smartalecsander boasted. "I've been making free calls all over the galaxy since I was in kindergarten."

"In that case, we've got a circuit for you to check out," Joke told him.

"Hey, fellas," Westerly said, "I don't think we should fool around with that equipment. It's the property of Milky Way Bell. We might get in trouble."

Eggnog pulled Joke aside and hissed, "We've gotta lose this dork."

"Yeah, but let's not just lose him," Joke whispered. "Let's make sure he stays lost. Play along with my plan." They turned back to the other pair.

"Westerly," Joke said, "you wanna see something neat in our security chief's office?"

"Sure!" Westerly said eagerly. Westerly and Smartalec-sander followed Joke and Eggnog to the shape-shifter's workroom. On the way there, Westerly managed to stumble through several puddles of radioactive waste in the mall and somehow picked up some tar on his shoe as well.

"Only three lumps of sugar in your tea, Yoohoo?" Counselor Deanna Troit inquired pleasantly.

Yoohoo nodded. "I'm watching my weight." Admiring the cup and saucer, she turned to Lt. Jazzy Fax. "What exquisite bone china you have, Jazzy," she said.

"Thank you," Jazzy said. "I got it at a rummage sale put on by a fellow Thrill who used to inhabit the body of an elderly socialite. His current host is a two-hundred-and-fifty-pound bricklayer who doesn't give many tea parties."

"Is it difficult adapting to a new lifestyle when your inner self acquires a new host body?" Troit asked.

"Not as hard as you'd think," said Jazzy, offering them a tray of shortbread cookies. "The trickiest part is finding a suitable new job. For instance, when I got this body, I did a lot of fashion modeling before returning to a Starfreak assignment. Actually, it was kind of nice taking a detour in my career. The money was better in modeling."

Yoohoo downed a cookie in one gulp and commented,

"That must have been an exciting lifestyle."

"It was," Jazzy said, "but unfortunately the world of *haute couture* really spoiled me for life anywhere else—especially here on the station, where the fashions are *so* dreary."

"We'd noticed," Troit commented, "but we didn't want to say anything."

"Oh, Deanna, that wouldn't offend me. I know how ugly the outfits must look to you," Jazzy said. "I've asked Bungeeman to get a color consultant in here to do everyone's color seasons, but he says it's simply not in the budget. So all the uniforms are still those muddy 'autumn' colors. Ugh." Jazzy wrinkled her nose. "The outfits that Vera and Quirk wear are especially distressing. And not exactly flattering to their figures, either." She leaned toward them and added delicately, "Quirk ought to get himself a pair of control-top leggings."

Reaching for another cookie, Yoohoo said, "I've found that space travel in general can be really hard on one's looks."

"It is," Jazzy agreed. "The low humidity, the lack of sunshine . . . "

"—And the scarcity of really talented manicurists," Yoohoo offered. The other two nodded.

Yoohoo set down her teacup and gazed around Jazzy's parlor. "I love what you've done with your quarters," she said. Her glance alighted on an end table, which held a bright pink Barbie coloring book.

Noticing Yoohoo's interest in the book, Jazzy said, "That's the latest edition. I just got it yesterday and couldn't put it down all night." She beamed. "Barbie's my role model."

"Oh, so you read," Yoohoo said.

Jazzy hesitated. "Well, sort of."

"Then I'll have to give you a copy of my autobiography, *Beyond Belief*," Yoohoo offered. "It's newly published in

"I love what you've done with your quarters."

hardcover—the complete story of my richly detailed Star-freak career—almost nineteen pages long."

Jazzy's forehead wrinkled in a pretty little frown as she said, "I hope it has lots of pictures."

The door chime sounded, and Jazzy went to greet the caller at the door. It was Capt. Smirk.

"Captain," Jazzy said, blushing with pleasure. "What a nice surprise."

"You're looking gorgeous today, Lieutenant," Smirk said with a debonair smile. "I just came by to ask if you know where Mr. Smock is. He hasn't been around the station since Wednesday."

"I haven't seen him," Jazzy said. "Right now I'm entertaining Counselor Troit and Officer Yoohoo. Mr. Smock isn't here."

"Are you sure?" Smirk inquired lightly. "He might just be wandering through. Maybe we ought to check your bedroom."

Noticing that Jazzy didn't seem inclined to throw Smirk out of her quarters, Troit and Yoohoo rose, making polite noises about how it was time for them to leave anyway. "Oh, must you?" Jazzy asked half-heartedly. "Well, thanks for coming. We must do this again soon." The three women traded air kisses, and Troit and Yoohoo left. Yoohoo's swaying hips were exaggerated by the pocketsful of shortbread cookies she took with her.

Cmdr. Crisco grunted in disgust when Smiles O'Brine came by to tell him that the station's audio system was on the fritz again.

"I'm sorry, Commander," O'Brine said, "but I'll need your communicator pin. I'm collecting everybody's pins and taking them to my workshop."

Crisco surrendered his pin to O'Brine, griping, "That's five times in three months that these pins have stopped working. Can't you do a permanent repair?"

O'Brine shook his head. "They've never really perfected

the technology to make these cordless jobbies transmit
very well through a space station. There's too much metal
here." Pocketing Crisco's pin, he added, "Have you given
any thought to the idea I came up with the other day? I
think it's a pretty good alternative."

"Well, I don't," Crisco said. "Wearing clip-on micro-
phones and plugging them into a different console in every
room would be wildly impractical, Mr. O'Brine."

O'Brine shrugged. "Suit yourself," he said.

As O'Brine left the office, Crisco's phone rang. He glared
at it, annoyed at the need to resort to this clumsy system
again. Picking up the receiver, he barked, "Hello?"

Several minutes later, Crisco got a word in edgewise.
"Dr. Brassiere, would you get to the point? . . . A severe
stomachache? . . . No, we can't access Westerly's medical
records from the film school. The subspace communicator
is broken again. . . . You can't perform any surgery without
his mother's permission. Hold on a minute. I'll find her."

Crisco consulted the computer readout on his credenza,
then muttered "Confound it!" and went back to the phone.
"Brassiere, I forgot—Dr. Flusher is missing. Don't go
ahead with Westerly's surgery until I locate her. Crisco
out—uh, I mean, goodbye." He hung up the phone.

Crisco walked out to the middle of the Sloperations
Command Center and stood there wondering what to do
next. He decided he'd try to dump the whole mess in Dodo's
lap. It seemed vaguely like a Security matter, anyway.

He reached up to tap his communicator pin, realized it
was gone, and stepped over to Fax's vacant workstation to
use her pink Princess phone. After dialing Dodo's exten-
sion, he let the phone ring a dozen times before giving up.

Crisco walked down the Promenade, hoping to run into
Dodo or somebody else who might provide some clues. Up
ahead he noticed two officers wearing the uniforms of Capt.
Smirk's crew. One of them was collaring passersby and
demanding, "Excuse me. Ve are looking for a nuclear wessel. Can you help us?" The other stood a few feet away;

he also looked lost but apparently was too embarrassed to ask directions.

"Perhaps I can help you," Crisco said to the pair. "I'm Bungeeman Crisco, commander of this station."

The officers introduced themselves as Checkout and Zulu of Smirk's *Endocrine*. Crisco apologized for not having had anyone meet them at the shuttlebay dock, and gave them directions to the guest quarters.

As the two officers walked away, Crisco spotted his son Joke. Crisco's temper flared as he saw that Joke was still hanging around with that troublemaker Eggnog, and with some Kringle boy, too.

Crisco sneaked up on the three, who were having a good laugh about something. He grabbed his son by the ear and cried, "Gotcha!" The other two squealed in alarm and ran away.

"Dad, lemme go!" Joke yiped.

"Not until you tell me what you've been up to, young man," Crisco said.

"Ouch! That's the same spot Dodo pinches every day," Joke protested as Crisco squeezed his ear a little tighter. "Daaad—we were just having fun, that's all."

"At whose expense this time?" Crisco demanded.

"Ow oww owww—Westerly Flusher!" Joke cried.

Crisco's suspicion turned to alarm as he remembered the call from Dr. Brassiere in Sick Bay. "What did you do to him?" Crisco growled.

"We were just fooling around," Joke said. "Dodo was resting in his quarters. You know, sitting in that pail he uses—"

"When he shape-shifts into a glob of oatmeal," Crisco said, finishing Joke's sentence for him.

"Yeah. Well, we showed it to Westerly and dared him to eat it." Joke cringed, as if expecting his father to whack him upside the head at any moment. "Except we sorta left out the part about the oatmeal being Dodo. So Westerly ate it. I mean, he ate him."

"Excuse me. Ve are looking for a nuclear wessel."

"We showed it to Westerly and dared him to eat it."

Crisco's expression twisted in a tempest of anger and horror. "You mean Dodo is inside Westerly's stomach right now?"

"Gee, Dad, it was just a joke. We didn't think Westerly would go through with it. We had no idea that he actually *likes* oatmeal," Joke whined.

There was a phone booth a few steps away. Crisco dashed for it—pulling Joke by the ear—and dialed Sick Bay. Waiting for someone to answer the call, Crisco scolded his son: "Westerly was complaining of abdominal pain. Let's hope Dodo doesn't expand out of his resting state while he's still inside Westerly's stomach." Joke scowled.

"Hello?" Crisco returned his attention to the phone as someone came on the line. He blurted out, "Dr. Brassiere, listen: I just found out that Westerly has eaten Dodo . . . yes, that's what I said—so you'll probably want to induce vomiting at once. Maybe you can do that Jolly Green Giant routine of yours for him. . . . "

As Crisco paused to catch his breath, Brassiere's voice crackled faintly through the receiver. "What?" Crisco said. "Dodo has already left Westerly's body? How? . . . *Egads*. I'm coming right over, Doctor. Don't do anything until I get there. And for heaven's sake, don't flush."

Yawns filled the guest quarters as the newcomers straggled into their rooms that night. Troit and Yoohoo yawned, exhausted from the rigors of Jazzy's tea party. Zulu and Checkout yawned; being nonentities on the space station was even tougher than being nonentities on Smirk's ship. Smartalecsander yawned, tired yet happy from showing off his budding criminal personality to his new hoodlum friends. And Westerly yawned, wiped out after a day of making medical history.

The final yawn came after they were all tucked into their beds in the dark, when the void yawned open again, ripping the muted-plaid fabric of space and drawing them into a mysterious dimension where no one but their ill-fated crewmates had gone before.

5

Readin', Rattin'
and 'Rithmetic

EVENING CAME, and morning followed—but much later this time, for it was Saturday, and everybody slept late.

At midmorning, Capt. Smirk went window-shopping on the Promenade. He'd just stopped to check out the display at Tribble Taxidermy ("You fluff 'em, we stuff 'em") when Capt. Ricardo came trotting up.

"Thank goodness I've found you," Ricardo said, panting from his dash down the hall. "We've got to talk. It's urgent."

"Good grief—something important has happened and you're not going to convene a meeting about it?" Smirk needled him.

Ricardo frowned. "It's something you and I must handle alone."

They walked over to the saloon, which had a new neon sign: "Quirk's Sports Bar." At Ricardo's urging, they took a secluded table in a dark corner. After the waitress had left them alone with their beverages, Smirk asked, "So what's the big news?"

"I found out something at the tail end of a Viewscreen call to Admiral Gogetter a moment ago," Ricardo said. "I'd been trying to find out the details of this vacation perk he offered. Anyway, when we'd finished talking, he apparently thought he'd hung up—but he hadn't. I think he just hit the wrong button on his screen. You know how he's always doing several things at once."

"Several?" Smirk interjected. "More like a dozen. He's got the attention span of a flea."

Ricardo nodded and went on, "He started talking to his secretaries as if I wasn't listening, and you wouldn't believe what I heard." Ricardo shakily lifted the teacup to his lips and took a sip of Earl Grape to steady his nerves.

"Well, go on," Smirk urged. "Don't make me drag it out of you. This isn't one of those soap operas your crew is hooked on."

Ricardo set down the teacup and told him, "If we can't break this dullimia epidemic, Starfreak will simply cut off the payroll to our crews and direct those funds to the space station."

"What?!" Smirk cried. His exclamation caught the attention of some Tizzians at the nearest table, distracting them from their game of Spoons. Smirk leaned in closer to Ricardo and hissed, "You're kidding!"

Ricardo shook his head. "I wish I were. But it sounds as if Starfreak is willing to lavish extraordinary resources on the station at the expense of the rest of the fleet."

"But—but—" Smirk sputtered, "these guys don't deserve it. They're so pedestrian. Who cares what happens to them in the long run?"

"Starfreak does," Ricardo answered. "Admiral Gogetter's words were: 'We're gonna throw dough at them until they rise to the occasion.' "

"Uhhhnnn." Smirk covered his face with his hands. Neither of them said anything for a few moments. The only sound was the ball clicking against levers at the foosball table.

Eventually, Smirk peeked out from between his hands and asked, "Does Gogetter know that our crewmembers have disappeared?"

"No," Ricardo said. "And I don't think we should tell

They took a secluded table in a dark corner.

him, either. He'd probably give up on us immediately if he knew."

Smirk stared glumly at the opposite corner, where four Zirconians were playing Pegs. Finally he said, "Well, Jean-Lucy, I hate to say it, but you and I will have to work together till the end on this one."

Ricardo nodded, acknowledging the painful truth.

"First things first," Smirk said. Having made up his mind, he began to bounce back from the shock, and he sat up straighter. "We've got to find our missing crewmembers so they can finish this coaching thing. And not just for coaching—I'd sort of like to have them back on my ship when this is all over."

Ricardo agreed, "So would I. Can you imagine what it would be like to live all alone on a starship? For one thing, who would tend bar in Ten-Foreplay?"

Their conversation was interrupted as a rugby ball landed on the table. A player dashed up, apologized, threw the ball away, and managed to run three steps beyond the table before getting flattened by a herd of opponents.

"We need to pressure Crisco to find out what's happened to our people," Smirk said. "We'll give him an ultimatum: start hustling, or we'll immediately tell Starfreak Command that our crewmembers have disappeared."

"But we wouldn't tell that to Starfreak Command," Ricardo countered. "We don't want them to know that our crews are gone."

"Yes, but we can still use it as a bluff. Crisco doesn't know we know they're not supposed to know," Smirk said. "For all we know, he might not even know what they know about this, much less what we know."

As Ricardo tried following Smirk's logic, his eyes started to cross. Smirk punched him lightly on the shoulder. "You're going to have to trust me on this, Jean-Lucy," he said. When Ricardo looked hesitant, Smirk added, "I was already dealing in office politics when you were still knee-high to a pattern buffer."

* * *

A half-hour later, Smirk and Ricardo loomed over Crisco's desk, and Smirk demanded, "Well, Commander, I hope you've come up with a better idea for finding our missing crewmembers."

"Yes, Captain. I figure that somebody on the station has to have seen something," Crisco said. "A few of them may even be responsible for the disappearances. I've ordered all my key staff and any civilians involved in the coaching sequence to report to the classroom at 1100 hours. We'll pry the truth out of them one way or another."

The office door swooshed open, and Dodo entered. "You wanted me, Commander?" he asked.

"Yes, Dodo," said Crisco. "I need you to stand guard at this meeting in case things get ugly." Dodo nodded and followed them out of the room.

As they walked down the hall, Capt. Ricardo said to Dodo, "I heard what happened with you and Westerly Flusher. Have you fully recovered?"

"Well, I showed up for work this morning because I couldn't afford to take a sick day, even though I still feel like sh— . . . uh, I'm not quite back up to par," Dodo revealed.

While Dodo and Ricardo walked a few steps ahead, Smirk murmured to Crisco, "What about Dodo? Isn't he under suspicion, too?"

"Captain Smirk," Crisco said icily, "Dodo is my chief of Security. I trust him implicitly." After a pause, he admitted, "Besides, Dodo could shape-shift right out of any detention cell we could devise. I've given this a lot of thought since arriving at the station, believe me." Crisco rolled his eyes in a gesture of futility. "If he *were* guilty, how would you punish him?"

"You could take away his pail," Smirk suggested.

"Hmmm." Crisco grew pensive. "I never thought of that."

As they continued walking through the station, Crisco

told the captains that this meeting was being held in the classroom because it was the largest room with seating. Smiles O'Brine's wife Kookoo had set up a school there, the station's first.

Unfortunately for the cause of higher education, classes had been suspended the day before, pending a court order. A suit had been brought by a parents' organization, STODGY (Stop Teaching Our Descendants Garbage, Y'all), protesting a sex-education class in which Kookoo had handed out condoms to the human students and stocking caps to the Ferengi youngsters.

"What makes you think anybody will show up for this meeting, Crisco?" Capt. Smirk asked as the four of them entered the classroom. "People around here don't exactly jump whenever you snap your fingers."

Crisco flipped some switches on the wall, and fluorescent lights flickered on overhead. "They'll come," he predicted. "Chief O'Brine finished repairing their communicator pins, and if they want them back, they'll have to pick them up at this meeting."

Sure enough, this tactic got Crisco a full turnout. O'Brine handed out pins to everyone as they came in the door: first Jazzy Fax and Dr. Brassiere, then Quirk, then Joke and Eggnog, and finally Major Vera.

They sat behind the metal schooldesks. The adults squirmed, trying to get comfortable in the little chairs, while Crisco wrote the names of Smirk's and Ricardo's missing crewmembers on the blackboard. Dodo guarded the door, scanning the group intently as if expecting someone to draw a phaser at any moment.

Crisco finished writing, brushed his palms together to wipe off the chalk dust, and turned to the group.

"Every one of these crewmembers has arrived here at Geek Space Nine since Wednesday," he announced, "and every one of them has disappeared. I find this rather curious."

He paced the aisles slowly, glaring down at the heads

of his fellow space station residents. "Now, I'm not naming any names, but certain people in this room are known to resent the idea of being coached by the starship personnel," Crisco said. "Something tells me that these people had a hand in their disappearance."

Crisco's pacing returned him to the front of the room. Steepling his fingers in front of his face for a moment, he paused, giving the group a judgmental look. Then he invited, "If the guilty parties step forward now and tell what they did, they won't get hurt. Much."

Crisco waited, pressing his lips together in a tight little frown. The only sound in the room was the buzz of the fluorescent lights.

"People," Crisco warned, "I'm starting to lose patience with you." The silence continued.

Ricardo and Smirk walked to the door, and Crisco followed them out into the hall.

As soon as the door closed behind them, Capt. Smirk said, "I'm getting fed up with this, Crisco. I want my crew back, or Starfreak is going to hear just how incompetent you are at running this station." Capt. Ricardo seconded that emotion with a glare, and the two captains walked away.

Crisco returned to the room and stood before the group. Sternly he demanded, "Okay, out with it. Let's have the truth." Nobody made a sound. Crisco folded his arms over his chest and barked, "Let's hear it!" No one volunteered.

Finally he snapped, "All right, if you want to play it that way—I've got plenty of time. You'll all sit here serving detention until somebody squeals."

Crisco yanked out the chair behind the teacher's desk and huffily sat himself down. Determined to make good use of the time, he started correcting a pile of papers Kookoo O'Brine had left on the desktop. Meanwhile, Dodo shapeshifted into a hawk and crouched on the sill of the transom window above the door, peering down at the group.

No one came forward to confess. Hours passed. Eggnog,

No one came forward to confess. Hours passed.

who happened to be sitting at the desk he used when he occasionally showed up for class, pulled out his copy of *Playlobe* magazine. He hid the magazine behind a textbook and gazed at the centerfold.

Dr. Brassiere put his head down on his desk, and soon he began snoring softly. Jazzy Fax filed her nails. Smiles O'Brine sketched a drag racer on the cover of a notebook.

Major Vera scribbled a note on a piece of lined paper and folded it into a triangle. She waited till Dodo was looking the other way, then passed the note down the rows and out of the room. It was addressed to one of her Bridge-oran pals.

Moments later, the phone rang on the teacher's desk. Crisco answered it, listened to the caller, sighed, and hung up.

"All right, everybody clear the room," he said. "Someone just called in a bomb threat."

6

Eggsistential
Philosophy

EVENING CAME, and morning followed. And since it was Sunday morning, the search for the missing personnel had to be put on hold; Bridgeorans would not allow anyone to work before noon on the Sabbath. Not that the station's residents used the time off to follow religious observances—most of them simply slept late for the second day in a row and waited for the stores to open—but the custom lingered nonetheless.

One of the few on the space station who did observe the Sabbath was Major Vera. The ritual began when she turned on the television in her quarters.

The broadcast originated from the planet where the Bridgeorans' spiritual leader, the ChiroPractor, lived in exile; she owned a condo next door to the Dalai Lama.

The planet was on the other side of the wormhole, in the Gummi Quadrant. Every Bridgeoran schoolchild could recite the tale of how the ChiroPractor had gotten stuck there. She'd been touring the area in a shuttlecraft with several residents of the space station when she'd felt a mysterious compulsion to visit a hazardous planet known to the locals as East L.A. Down on the surface, the ChiroPractor had been caught between rival gangs in a drive-by shooting. When the ChiroPractor died, Major Vera had bawled so loudly that she could be heard on the other side of the wormhole.

Then, shockingly, the ChiroPractor had sprung back to life. Dr. Brassiere, examining her and some natives who'd also returned from the dead, found that the planet itself caused metabolic changes—a mysterious chemical reaction in the bloodstream related to the plotting factor.

The bottom line was that if the ChiroPractor ever tried to leave the planet, she would suffer a severe case of the bends and explode all over the inside of any shuttlecraft foolish enough to offer her a ride. Bridgeorans fervently hoped that a cure would someday be found for this condition so the ChiroPractor could safely return to them. Medical research was ongoing yet poorly funded—practically every store countertop on her home planet had a coin cannister marked "GIVE So the ChiroPractor May LIVE (on Badger)." Meanwhile, the Bridgeorans living on Badger had to make do with spiritual sustenance via satellite.

Today was Earster Sunday, when Bridgeorans celebrated the ChiroPractor's resurrection by setting out baskets full of candy ear-chains for the children and telling them stories about the Earster bunny.

As the television broadcast began, Vera watched the opening credits. The words scrolled over live shots of a crowd assembled in a plaza on East L.A. In front of the people loomed an imposing cathedral where the ChiroPractor hung out on Sundays. The camera, scanning the walls of the cathedral, moved up slowly and dramatically till it reached the rooftop chimney.

A puff of white smoke emerged from the chimney, prompting cheers from the assembly; it was the signal that the ChiroPractor had just finished breakfast and tossed the crusts of her toast into the fireplace.

Soon the ChiroPractor emerged onto a balcony of the cathedral, where she could be seen by all in the crowd. She favored her listeners with some dippy New Age sayings,

Bridgeorans celebrated by telling stories about the
Earster bunny.

prompting warm and fuzzy feelings in all who were faithful enough to suspend common sense.

Next came a hymn, "Earer My God to Thee." Vera didn't like to sing, and this part of the service always bored her. She flipped through the hymnal, amusing herself by reading hymn titles and mentally adding the phrase "under the bedcovers" after each of them.

She began watching the broadcast again as the hymn ended and one of the deacons opened the Sacred Appliance Garage in the cathedral's foyer. He brought out an urn containing a relic known as the Tear of the Profit. The faithful Bridgeorans standing in the plaza began to bawl on cue.

Then there was the collection. As the camera showed plates being passed around the crowd for contributions of gold-pressed laudanum, an 800 number and the message "all major credit cards accepted" were superimposed for the television audience.

Vera had already made her quarterly pledge, so once again she turned her attention from the screen.

To kill some time during the collection, Vera scanned the Sunday bulletin she'd received in the mail. Although advertising was officially banned from the bulletin, there were ways around that. Ferengi businesses, in particular, were adept at finding loopholes. Today's bulletin said that the cathedral's altar flowers had been given "in honor of Dogbreath Construction, specializing in corrugated cardboard siding. Call 1-800-RIP-OFFF for a free estimate."

The collection ended. After a few more words of wisdom from the ChiroPractor, the organist struck up the last hymn. However, few of the parishioners in the plaza joined in this time, since they were already impatient for the service to end. They craned their necks to see the ChiroPractor walk back into the cathedral and disappear from their view. At that moment, protocol allowed the people to leave. They raced for their cars, hoping to avoid being caught in a jam out in the parking lot.

Vera switched off her television and sat for a moment with her eyes closed, basking in the glow of spiritual renewal. Then she went out to the Promenade to buy the Sunday paper and some sweet rolls.

Re-entering her quarters, Vera felt a sudden suspicion that she was not alone. *The last time I had this feeling, it turned out that Dodo was spying on me,* she recalled. From her bathroom cabinet she retrieved a plastic shaker of talcum powder and began sprinkling it around the living room.

Hearing several violent sneezes, Vera traced them to the far wall, where a curio cabinet displayed her collection of porcelain poodle figurines. She sprinkled more powder over the unit and watched carefully. Another sneeze revealed that Dodo was on the top shelf, disguising himself as her Thighmaster. Vera realized that Dodo had been sitting there all morning. Now he expanded back into his tall humanoid shape, nearly breaking the cabinet in the process.

"Well, I hope you're satisfied, Dodo," jeered Major Vera. "You caught me red-handed watching a church service."

"I'm just trying to find out what's happened to our missing persons," Dodo said, sniffing as the talcum powder continued to tickle his sinuses. "I thought some of you might give yourselves away in an unguarded moment. Unfortunately, you're all too suspicious." He pulled a doily off the cabinet and blew his nose in it.

Vera rolled up her sleeves and prepared to usher him out the door. Dodo took the hint and hurried out under his own power, commenting, "I've got half a mind to outlaw talcum powder on this station. Just once, I'd like to complete a surveillance without being sprinkled."

When Capt. Smirk and Capt. Ricardo turned up in Cmdr. Crisco's office on Sunday evening demanding a progress report, Crisco had to admit that the investigation was no further along than before.

Capt. Smirk hinted darkly that he might be interested in taking over Crisco's job at the station. Starfreak Command would probably let him, Smirk added, "especially since I'm succeeding so well in our current mission."

Crisco looked skeptical. "I haven't noticed my people showing any more dimensionality than usual," he countered.

"I've been making great progress—with Jazzy Fax, at least," Smirk claimed. "She's shown me some unbelievable aspects of her ... uh ... personality."

"Commander Crisco," Capt. Ricardo broke in, "we've looked everywhere on this station for our crewmembers, with no success. Perhaps it's time to call in Lieutenant Commander Dacron."

"Your android?" Crisco said with a frown.

"He has taken on a Sherlock Holmes persona in our HolidayDeck many times," Ricardo went on, "and successfully solved a few mysteries for us."

"I don't know if I can stand having him around," Crisco said. "He really rubbed me the wrong way when we met."

"If he gets on your nerves, you can always press his 'reset' button," Ricardo said. "It provides a marvelous sense of catharsis, and he never knows what hit him."

"I say that if he can solve our problem, let's get him over here," Smirk stated. "Have you got any better ideas, Crisco?"

"No," Crisco admitted. "All right, Captain Ricardo, bring your android in on the case."

His shoulders sagging, Crisco entered the quarters he shared with Joke. He had worked for hours without success on the dilemma of the missing persons, and the stress was getting to him. It was time for a diversion.

Crisco trudged to the doorway of his son's room. Joke was stretched out on the bed writing in a workbook. Crisco felt a flicker of hope when he noticed that the workbook was the SAT study guide he'd given Joke, but the flicker

died as he drew closer and saw that Joke was simply filling
in the centers of all the "o's" with his pencil.

"Hey, Joke," Crisco said, "how'd you like to join me in
the Hollowsweets for a game of baseball?"

"Aww, I'm too tired, Dad," Joke said, "and I'm sore,
too." He reached for the back of his right thigh and rubbed
his hamstring muscle. "I tried out a new Hollowsweets
program yesterday—a track meet."

"Well, all right. We don't have to play. We can just have
a cozy father-son chat," Crisco said, sitting in the chair at
Joke's desk. "Say, how about those Brewers, huh? Did you
see the stats on yesterday's game?" Joke shrugged and went
back to filling in the circles. "I know," Crisco said, "let's
see which one of us can remember the most RBI statistics
without looking in the record book. You first."

"Dad," Joke whined, setting down his pencil, "if there's
anything more boring than watching baseball, it's talking
about baseball."

"Since when?" Crisco demanded. "Joke, you used to like
baseball."

"That was *yesterday*," Joke said in a tone that gave the
word its teenage connotation: ancient history.

"But son, baseball players stand for everything that's
noble and wonderful about the human race."

"What, that people are capable of standing around grabbing their crotches and spitting tobacco juice?" Joke retorted. "Or do you mean the way they scream at the
umpire? Or throw beanballs? Or spike their opponents
when sliding into base?"

"No, no," Crisco said, becoming increasingly frustrated.
"I mean in a larger sense. The game of baseball is a met-
aphor for life."

"Yeah, that's for sure," Joke said. "A few overpaid people
grab all the glory while the other schmucks stand around
waiting for a hit that never comes to their section of the
field."

Crisco said sharply, "You've got one bad attitude there,

boy. What kind of phys ed classes was Kookoo O'Brine conducting before the school shut down?"

"We didn't exactly have phys ed," Joke said. "We were learning to play Bridge."

"Bridge?!"

"Yeah. Mrs. O'Brine told us, 'When in Badger, do as the Bridgeorans do.' "

"Bridge is too sedentary to be your main recreation," Crisco countered.

"That's why I tried out the track program in the Hollowsweets, Dad. Baseball is so lame. I wanted to see what it feels like to actually get in shape."

"Joke, I'd much prefer you stick with baseball. It teaches you good old-fashioned values like teamwork. Track won't give you that. There's too much emphasis on individual performance." Joke scowled, but Crisco pressed his point: "It doesn't really matter to your track teammates how well you do."

Joke gave his father a disdainful look and told him, "Obviously you've never dropped the baton in a four-by-one-hundred-meter relay."

" . . . So you and I should coach the others, too, not just Commander Crisco, while Dacron looks for our missing crewmembers," said Capt. Ricardo. "At the very least, we could coach Crisco's key Sloperations people. Don't you agree, Captain Smirk?"

"Hmmm," Smirk said idly, staring at a voluptuous Troglodyte lounging against the railing of Quirk's second-floor balcony.

"Captain, have you heard a word I've said?" Ricardo asked with a frown. "I thought that at least you'd be able to pay attention until Lieutenant Fax arrives."

"I heard you," Smirk said evenly. "You think that expanding the coaching will give us a head start until Dacron finds our crews. Right?"

"Uh, yes, that's correct," said Ricardo, mollified.

"I dunno, Jean-Lucy," Smirk said. He sipped his cola, glanced at the entrance for the tenth time, and wondered aloud, "What's taking Jazzy so long? Does it really take more than an hour to get an herbal-mud-pack facial?"

Capt. Ricardo turned peevish. "I thought we'd agreed that it's essential to work together on this project," he said. "You seem to be losing interest in our dilemma."

"Not really," Smirk said, measuring the Troglodyte with his eyes. "I just don't want to get more involved in coaching. It's boring enough just to coach Crisco. Taking on any more people would really make my allergy flare up, and I'm almost out of Seldane."

The Troglodyte sauntered away from the balcony. Smirk turned back to Ricardo and added, "I say we take care of things one at a time. We locate our crewmembers, so they can help with the coaching, so we can get on with conquering new worlds and new women."

"In that case, it seems that the next stage depends on Dacron," Ricardo said, "since everyone else has been unable to locate our crewmembers." Smirk nodded in agreement.

Ricardo thought for a moment, then added, "I think Dacron has become wary after being the butt of so many practical jokes lately. He may cooperate more fully if he thinks he can trust us. May I suggest that you refrain from making fun of him on this assignment?"

"Oh, excuuuuuse me," Smirk retorted. "I'm not the one who just suggested to Crisco that we flick Dacron's 'reset' switch to provide a little comic relief."

"All right, so my crew has taken out our frustration on him occasionally," Ricardo admitted, "but as his captain, I make it a point never to laugh in his face."

"Okay. I'll play along with that," Smirk said, "to get him to work harder. If you can keep a straight face when he's around, so can I."

Ricardo noticed that the Ferengi bartender, Quirk, was

pointing them out to an alien with two heads. A moment later, the alien approached their table.

"Excuse me," said the left head. "I heard you two are in charge of the crew-coaching operation going on here. I'm a sales representative for Virgil Reality, Inc. We make fight-or-flight simulators. They're used for training crews to react to a variety of emergency situations on starships and space stations. Our quality control is second to none, and our manufacturing facility—"

"Never mind that," interrupted the right head. "Sell the benefits! Gentlemen, our state-of-the-art unit provides complete turn-key coaching practice with minimal management input needed. Simply plug it in at any Bridge or Sloperations console, and it does the rest: simulating all aspects of a genuine emergency while you sit back and critique the reaction of personnel. If you order today, I'll throw in for no extra charge our videotape option, which records the entire experience for later review by your students."

"Sounds great," responded Capt. Smirk. "Do you take MasterCard?"

"Say," said the left head, "we skipped the part about the unit's non-glare, fingerprint-resistant monitor screen."

"Forget the screen!" said the right head. "Let's close the sale, you plodding sequentialist!" He pulled out an order form.

The sales-heads gave Smirk a carbonless copy of his order and promised to deliver the unit to the Sloperations Command Center within the hour.

"Say, this oughta be fun," Smirk said. He swallowed the rest of his cola. "I'll get to see how Jazzy behaves on the job." Crunching an ice cube between his teeth, Smirk added, "Shouldn't Dacron be here by now? He knows how badly we need him, doesn't he?"

Ricardo nodded. "I told him that this was urgent, and that he'll be taking on the persona of an investigator to search for our crew."

Noticing that people were turning to stare at the entrance to the bar, Smirk and Ricardo also looked at the door and saw Dacron walking in—wearing a dress.

Captain Ricardo grimaced at the sight of his second officer. Dacron's neck looked even gawkier than usual, sprouting from a scalloped neckline and emphasized by a choker. Cap sleeves stuck out at his shoulders. Beneath the shirtwaist, soft folds of flowered fabric billowed in a wide knee-length skirt, and Dacron's skinny white limbs stuck out beneath it. Ricardo wondered if he'd ever again be able to enjoy frog legs at his favorite French restaurant.

Dacron spotted the captains and began walking toward their table. Capt. Ricardo pressed his fingers to his temple and stared at the ceiling, trying to pretend he had nothing to do with this apparition that had managed to out-alienize every alien in Quirk's bar, where weirdness was the norm.

Capt. Smirk seemed about to launch into a laughing fit at any second. He held a fist to his pursed lips and turned scarlet, his eyes filling with tears from the flood of hilarity bubbling behind them.

"Good afternoon, Captain Ricardo, Captain Smirk," Dacron said with a polite nod to each of them. Lowering his head, Smirk pressed his fist harder against his mouth and managed to waggle his fingers at Dacron. His shoulders shook.

Forced to acknowledge Dacron's presence, Ricardo stared, aghast, as if he'd just seen Marley's ghost again. His voice faint, almost plaintive, Ricardo inquired, "Dacron, why are you wearing a dress?"

"You had asked me to assume an investigator's persona in my search for the missing crewmembers," Dacron explained. "I am tired of playing Sherlock Holmes. This time I have decided to take on the identity of Nancy Drew."

"I suppose you're all wondering why I've asked you to assemble here today," Capt. Ricardo said to those forming

Ricardo grimaced at the sight of his second officer.

a semicircle around him and Capt. Smirk in the Sloperations Command Center.

"Not really," Major Vera remarked. "Most of us work here, so we were already here before you asked for us."

"Uh, yes." Ricardo noticed that the others—Cmdr. Crisco, Jazzy Fax, Smiles O'Brine, Dodo and Dr. Julio Brassiere—also looked decidedly uncurious. "Well, be that as it may," he continued, "I wanted to let you know that my second officer, Dacron, is busy investigating the disappearance of our starship crews. Meanwhile . . . "

"Meanwhile," Capt. Smirk cut in, noticing that yawns were already appearing in their small audience, "we've got an action-packed simulation for you. This baby here—" he tapped the laminated top of the Virgil Reality Fight-or-Flight Simulator "—brings coaching into the twenty-fourth century. Let's plug it in and get going."

There was a short delay because the unit's three-pronged safety plug wouldn't fit into any of the five-holed outlets the Carcinogens had installed. Smiles O'Brine hunted through his junk drawer till he found an adaptor.

As soon as the unit was switched on, its readout indicated that it was establishing an interface with the Sloperations Center's computer. A few moments later, the LED panel signaled READY, and the unit began to spool forth a long paper printout.

"This hard copy describes some of the emergency situations that can be simulated," Ricardo told the group. "The unit formulated them on the basis of your databanks, personnel records, mission logs and so on."

When the machine finished printing, Ricardo tore the paper at its perforated edge. He and Smirk scanned the readout.

Simulations available for
Geek Space Nine personnel
—The wormhole is expanding, threatening to destroy the space station.

—The wormhole is contracting, threatening to destroy the space station.

—The wormhole is stable, for once, and everybody is worried: "It's awfully quiet out there." " . . . Yeah, too quiet."

—A Bridgeoran terrorist asks Vera to help him paint gang graffiti on the walls of the wormhole.

—The latest strain of the Hong Kong flu turns everyone's speech into Pig Latin.

—A mysterious anomaly thrusts Commander Crisco into the presence of aliens who exist outside linear time, thereby allowing him to re-create a baseball diamond that lures Shoeless Joe Jackson out of the cornfield.

—A mysterious anomaly brings the crew's fantasies to life, putting everyone else in danger of death by boredom.

—A mysterious anomaly coinciding with a visit from Q-Tip and Capt. Ricardo's girlfriend Stosh manages to make them look as stale as the regulars.

—A mysterious anomaly dies of overwork.

—The station's officers become pawns in an alien board game, "Barbie, Queen of the Prom," and are threatened by a rampaging Ken.

—Dodo thinks he has met another shape-shifter but is disappointed to learn that the mercurial creature is merely a humanoid descendant of Bill Clinton.

—Bridgeoran villagers mistake Smiles O'Brine for Moses and expect him to save them by parting the Red Herring.

—Political intrigue almost becomes Quirk's undoing when he is named to succeed the Ferengi's leader, the Grand Naugahyde.

—Lt. Jazzy Fax is accused of a 200-year-old littering misdemeanor allegedly committed by her previous host, but charges are dropped when the DA's office discovers that the evidence has rotted away.

Political intrigue almost becomes Quirk's undoing.

—Trapped in an elevator during his regeneration cycle, Dodo is saved when Ambassador Woksauna Troit cradles his gelatinous form in her bra.

—Smiles O'Brine adopts a "puppylike" space probe and allows it to reside in a computer subprogram until he discovers that it hasn't been housebroken yet.

The list went on and on. Smirk jumped ahead to read some of the fresher ideas. "Hey," he said, pointing to a line, "I like this one: 'Giant egg appears in middle of Sloperations Command Center.' Seems appropriate, Crisco. Obviously, *somebody* laid an egg here, or your space station wouldn't be in such trouble in the first place."

Ignoring Crisco's glare, Smirk entered the parameters of his chosen scenario into the simulator's keyboard. Another paper printout emerged from the machine; Ricardo tore it off and set it aside. He and Smirk each took a chair at the edge of the room.

Within moments, a giant egg materialized in the middle of the floor. "Okay, everybody," Smirk said, pointing to the egg, "pretend that this is just another day on the job, and react the way you would in an everyday emergency. I want to see your best bold-space-pioneer stuff. Action!"

Crisco's people gathered around the egg and got to work.

Major Vera became hyper in an instant. "Where did that thing come from?" she asked belligerently. "I don't like this. That's not a Bridgeoran egg." She thrust her face to within an inch of its smooth surface and demanded, "Who said you could come here?"

Jazzy Fax glanced at the egg and then moved to her science station. Studying the panels, she reported, "I'm getting dangerously high yolk pressure readings, Bungeeman. Six-hundred fifty-seven p.s.i. . . . seven-hundred seventy-eight p.s.i. . . . nine-hundred eighty-nine p.s.i. . . . the top could blow any minute."

Dr. Brassiere ran his prycorder over the eggshell, lis

tened to the egg with a stethoscope for a few moments, and then announced, "It's definitely a life form. It's also a very, very old egg. Therefore it's probably extremely sulfurous. If it does blow, it could stink up the entire station."

Smiles O'Brine folded his arms defiantly across his chest. "I suppose you expect me to fix this egg right away, huh? Well, you're gonna have to issue a work order and wait your turn. There are six repairs scheduled ahead of this one." He pulled a wrench from the pocket of his overalls and clanged it against a metal railing, yelling, "Nothin' works around this bloody place!"

Dodo circled the egg warily. He hooked a pocket-sized lie detector unit onto the shell. When the unit's readout flashed INNOCENT, he grunted skeptically, shape-shifted into an egg cozy, and draped himself over the intruder, the better to perform surveillance.

Crisco clucked his tongue at the others' reactions. In a mild tone he chided, "People, I think this calls for a little more understanding and tolerance. We could learn a lot from this egg."

"Hold it! Hold it!" Capt. Smirk called. He jumped up from his chair and strode to the center. "Is this really the best you guys can do?"

They looked puzzled. "You said to react the way we would in an everyday crisis, Captain," Dr. Brassiere said. "That's just what we were doing."

"But it's all so . . . so . . . predictable!" Smirk sputtered.

"I must agree," Ricardo said, joining Smirk in the center of the group. Ricardo showed them the readout that the simulator had printed at the beginning of the scenario. "All of your reactions were predicted by the machine," Ricardo said, "right down to the very words you've spoken."

Crisco scanned the readout. Sure enough, there was everything they'd said, printed word for word before they'd said it: "I'm getting dangerously high yolk pressure readings, Bungeeman." . . . "It's definitely a life form." . . .

"Nothin' works around this bloody place." . . . "We could learn a lot from this egg."

"It seems that we have our work cut out for us," Capt. Ricardo observed. "Now that we've established a baseline, let's run the simulation again. This time, everyone, please try to display more nuance in your reactions."

" 'Nuance'?" Dodo echoed.

"Right," Capt. Smirk seconded. "Instead of your usual stuff, give us something more subtle—something that shows us that you have more than one side to your personality."

"But we don't," Jazzy Fax said coolly, shrugging her shoulders.

"We know that, Lieutenant, but you can pretend you do," Capt. Ricardo explained. "That's how you develop character and exceed the limits of your dullimia. Understood?"

Everyone milled around, puzzling it over. Cmdr. Crisco said, "We *have* made some tentative forays into humor on a few occasions."

"Okay, humor. Humor is good. So throw in a couple of yuks," Smirk urged him. "What else?"

There was a long silence as everyone attempted to plumb the depths of their personalities or locate the depths in the first place.

Smirk drummed his fingers on the simulator for a minute, then said, "Never mind. We don't want to overanalyze this thing." He tapped instructions into the simulator's keyboard. The egg disappeared. "Let's just run the simulation again," Smirk told them, "only this time, try to act differently.

"Everybody ready?" Smirk said, pressing the "start" button. The simulated egg reappeared in the center of the floor. "Remember, do anything but your usual schtick. Okay, go!"

Crisco and his people gathered around the egg and stared

at it. Now that their standard reactions were taboo, they were obviously at a loss for what to do.

Two minutes later, Crisco finally spoke up. "Nice egg."

"Yes," Dr. Brassiere chimed in eagerly. "Very nice, indeed." After a long pause, he added, "It's very . . . egglike."

Dodo rasped, "This thing would make one heck of an omelette."

"Stop!" Capt. Smirk cried, holding a hand over his anguished face. "That's enough." He began searching his pockets. "Where's my antihistamine? I can feel a case of hives coming on."

Capt. Ricardo swatted his communicator insignia and said, "Ricardo to Lieutenant Commander Dacron." When the android responded, Ricardo continued, "Dacron, hurry up and find those missing crewmembers. Captain Smirk and I need their help as soon as possible. This coaching job is way too big for the two of us."

7

Monday,
Monday

EVENING CAME, and morning followed ... Monday—
ecchhh.
   *Second officer's personal log, Stardate 47805.0015
and three seconds. It is not easy being an android. My
efforts at creativity seem to be viewed as mere eccentricity.*

   *When I arrived at this space station yesterday after-
noon, Captain Ricardo failed to compliment my highly
authentic Nancy Drew costume and ordered me to change
back into uniform. He cited Starfreak regulations, but I
suspect that in reality he was jealous of the admiring looks
I drew from several patrons sitting at Quirk's bar.*

   *The investigation itself, which I completed yesterday
evening, was distinctly unchallenging. Deductive reason-
ing, coupled with routine inquiries, quickly revealed that
all of the missing persons had disappeared from the station's guest quarters within three successive nights. My
search of these quarters revealed the existence of a subspace distortion that has been tearing the fabric of space.
Specifically, it is a type of distortion known as a Talent
Void, or TV.*

   *A few measurements with the prycorder confirmed my
theory that as the members of the starship crews slept in
the guest quarters, they were sucked into the TV. Now*

*they remain suspended there, reduced to such a shallow
state that they are unable to move.*

*That same void is responsible for the dullimia epidemic
on this station. Laundry chutes link the guest quarters to
all other sleeping quarters, providing an energy conduit
for the void. This "slow leak" has been leeching the dimensionality out of the station's residents.*

*I avoided the guest quarters overnight and stayed in-
stead in one of Quirk's Hollowsweets with a recreation of
Yasha Tar from her pre-Romanumen era. We stayed up
until 0600 hours setting up dominoes to create a pattern
identical to the structure of the human DNA molecule,
and then knocking it over.*

*Now I am about to meet with Commander Crisco and
Captains Ricardo and Smirk to explain my findings.*

"*All* the guest quarters are on Level Sixteen?" asked Ricardo, echoing a fact Dacron had just mentioned. "Then
where have I been sleeping?"

"Please restate the question," responded the voice of the
station's computer.

"Never mind, Computer," Cmdr. Crisco said. Ricardo
glared at Crisco, suddenly understanding why his quarters
lacked certain amenities, like a bed.

Capt. Smirk grinned. "Gee, too bad I haven't gotten
around to spending the night in my assigned room." He
glanced through the glass panels of Crisco's office doors
toward Jazzy Fax's workstation. Jazzy sat at her console,
deeply engrossed in a fashion magazine, *Celebrity Freckle
Styles*.

Crisco asked Dacron, "How can we rescue those people
trapped in the void, Lieutenant?"

"I am afraid you cannot, Commander," Dacron answered. "It is much too dangerous for you, or anyone else
with dullimia, to enter the void. You, too, would become
trapped. Only someone with abundant dimensionality can

We stayed up until 0600 hours setting up
dominoes...

aid their escape. It will take several trips into the void for that person to escort everyone out."

Capt. Ricardo said knowingly to Dacron, "And you're about to volunteer for the job."

"Yes, Captain," Dacron said. He turned back to Crisco and continued, "In all modesty, Commander, I believe I have more dimensionality than all of your key people put together."

"Dacron, I can't let you do this," Ricardo said. "As your captain, I'm responsible for protecting you from undue risk. We know very little about this void; the mission would be too dangerous. We simply can't afford to lose you."

"I anticipated your objection, Captain," Dacron said, "and have already evaluated our options. Only one other officer has the personality range and depth to attempt this rescue: you."

"Hmmm. On the other hand, this mission might be a rewarding experience for you, Dacron," Ricardo said.

"Can't you both go?" Crisco inquired.

"Much as I'd love to," Ricardo said, tugging nervously at his tunic, "my contract with Starfreak specifically forbids hazardous practices like this, along with hang gliding, scuba diving, and eating hot chili peppers."

"I will begin the rescue attempt tomorrow afternoon," Dacron told them. "The TV distortion pattern undergoes cyclical fluctuations, and the computer indicates that the pattern will be at its lowest level during those hours. I will have only this one chance to get everyone out of the void before prime time reoccurs."

Captain's personal log, Stardate 47805.2. Dacron will attempt the rescue alone. He enters the void tomorrow afternoon.

Even though Dacron is our only hope, is it fair to ask him to take this risk? I find myself worrying whether he has enough dimensionality to survive repeated trips into the void. I wish there were someone here with whom I could blather on about the ethics of this matter—someone like Counselor Troit, or even Guano. Perhaps Dr. Brassiere could provide some guidance, or at least a referral.

"Philosophical issues?" Dr. Brassiere repeated blankly. "You mean like whether it's bad form to hit on Jazzy Fax more than once a day?"

"No," said Ricardo. "I'm worried about sending Dacron into battle, as it were, and I need a confidant who will listen to my qualms. It's something of a tradition for a captain to tour the ship before an engagement, you know, and get feedback from the galley slaves.

"I need someone who will discuss my fears," Ricardo went on, "and alleviate my guilt. Counselor Troit is good at that, since she has lots of psychobabble at her disposal. Guano, my chief bartender, is also quite adept. Somehow it's very helpful when Guano drops mysterious hints about our shared past or tells me 'Que serà, serà,' the way she did when the Bored were about to annihilate us. Isn't there someone like Troit or Guano here on the station—a professional adviser? A shoulder to cry on?"

Brassiere's expression conveyed as much depth of understanding as the stare of a gerbil. "I guess we don't have anyone who fills that role," he said. "Out here on the frontier, Captain, we just act. We don't think about it beforehand."

"I'll level with ya, guys," Admiral Gogetter said from the Viewscreen of the Sloperations Center late that evening. He'd called unexpectedly, asking to talk to all three senior officers at once. "We've got big trouble if you can't end this dullimia plague."

Smirk and Ricardo exchanged a glance. Crisco jutted out his chin and asked, "Could you be more specific, Admiral?"

"Big trouble," Gogetter specified. "Big, big trouble."

"You're referring just to the space station, right?" Smirk asked.

"No, not just the station," Gogetter said. "We're talking major down-the-tubes action—for the station *and* your crews, your starships, Starfreak Command, even the federation. The whole enchilada."

Gogetter shoved a piece of gum into his mouth as he riffled through his appointment calendar. "Oh, rats," he said, chewing loudly and talking to himself, "I meant to break up with Macy today." He cradled a phone receiver against his shoulder, punching touch-tone buttons as he shouted toward the reception area, "Mandy, while I'm calling Macy, would you get Marcy for me on line two?"

"Mandy has left for the night," an irritated female voice answered from the outer office. "So has Mindy."

Gogetter's index finger hovered over the phone. "Then who am I talking to?"

The secretary leaned into the office. "I'm Monday. You hired me today, remember? By the way, when do I get a lunch break? I haven't even had time to use the ladies' room since I started this morning."

"In a minute," Gogetter said as he went back to pushing phone buttons. "First I need you to get Marcy for me on line two. You'll find her number there in the Rolodex. It's under 'M.' "

"I figured that," Monday griped as she went back to her desk. "It's the only section this Rolodex has."

"Macy? Hi. It's Troy," Gogetter said into the phone. "Hey, baby, can you hold on for a minute?" After punching the "hold" button, he reached into his desk drawer and pulled out six white dinner plates and six skinny wooden rods. Gogetter stuck the rods into holes drilled in his desktop.

One by one, he balanced the plates on the tips of the rods and set them spinning. By the time he'd gotten the sixth one going, the first plate was starting to wobble;

quickly he spun it again and started back down the line, giving the others a whirl.

"Admiral," Cmdr. Crisco ventured via the Viewscreen, "I'm afraid I don't see the connection between our dullimia and the eventual downfall of the federation."

"It's like this," Gogetter said, pulling four rubber balls out of the center drawer of his desk. "My bosses laid it on the line this morning." He started juggling the balls. The plates kept spinning.

"The cost of restoring and keeping up your station has gotten totally out of control," Gogetter said. "I guess the High Command had no idea what a sinkhole that place is. They've taken out second, third, fourth and fifth mortgages on all Starfreak property to try to keep up." The first few plates began wobbling again; somehow Gogetter managed to restart them as he caught and tossed the four balls.

"Admiral, I've got Marcy for you on line two," Monday called.

"I'll get to her in a minute," Gogetter said, "after I break it off with Macy." With his eyes still fixed on the balls and the plates, Gogetter stabbed at the phone, hitting "speakerphone" and one of the line buttons. "Macy, listen," he said, "we both know it's not working out, so let's just call it quits, okay? No hard feelings? And hey, baby, can you send back the ring by courier before midnight? I need to use it again."

A rare silence descended on the office for a few moments. Then the voice from the speakerphone said, "This isn't Macy, it's Marcy. Apparently there's been someone else in your life, hmmm? Though it's obvious you weren't treating her very well."

"Oh, no," Gogetter groaned. "Wrong line. Wait, Marcy. I was just going to propose to you. I can explain—"

"Forget it, Troy," she barked. There was a loud *click*, followed by the drone of a dial tone.

Gogetter acknowledged the pain of breakup by biting his thumb for an instant. In the next second he switched off the speakerphone as he continued juggling and plate-spinning.

"So, Crisco," he said to the Viewscreen, "your station personnel have got to snap out of this dullimia. You've gotta be the hot new thing again. Heck, right now I'd be happy if you even managed to be the lukewarm new thing. Just be *something* that aliens will want to visit, so we can take in money and keep paying off the mortgages. Otherwise the space station will be reclaimed by the Carcinogens—"

"The Carcinogens?" Crisco cried.

"—And they'll also take the collateral Starfreak signed over," Gogetter said, "including the starships."

"Our starships?!" Ricardo and Smirk shrieked in unison.

Gogetter pulled the gum from his mouth and tossed it toward his heaping wastebasket, which was swarming with flies. "Hey, guys, take it easy," he told them. "I've got enough on my mind without you going to pieces on me. I'm telling you, this has been one rotten day. A typical Monday!" he hollered. "I hate Monday!"

Monday stomped into the office. "Oh, yeah? Well, the feeling is mutual!"

Gogetter turned toward her. "No, Monday, I didn't mean—"

A slowly spinning plate took a final wobble and then fell to the floor and shattered. Gogetter reached for the rod next to it, but that plate was also beyond saving, and it crashed. Then two of the juggling balls bounced off Gogetter's head. He reached toward the Viewscreen control button. "Gogetter out." The screen went blank.

8

Emotion in Motion

EVENING CAME, and morning followed . . . and shortly thereafter came Tues- day aaaafternoooon . . . In the middle of that afternoon, five officers assembled in the guest quarters in front of the Talent Void that Dacron had discovered. All but one of them were nervous.

Capt. Ricardo's rumpled face reflected a sleepless night; he'd been wrestling with his conscience about sending Dacron alone on this dangerous mission.

Capt. Smirk and Cmdr. Crisco looked jittery, since they knew that if Dacron blew the assignment, their own careers were in jeopardy.

Security Chief Dodo was afraid the others would expect him to perform a rescue if Dacron ran into trouble. The void sounded pretty tricky to him, and he doubted that jumping into it to save this foolish android and the other victims would be worth the risk.

Only Dacron appeared calm. He had spent the morning strolling along the Promenade, and the utter predictability of the happenings around the station had lulled him into a near-hypnotic state of tranquility.

Dacron tried pointing out to the others the exact location of the Talent Void, but they found it difficult to see. There was simply nothing there. It was just so very . . . void. It was as void as Checkout's personality . . . as void as the face of someone trying to talk to Chief Engineer Snot about the ship's engines without help from the Universal Translator . . . as void as Commander Piker's mind when he declared a Yellow Alert on the Bridge because the flyswatter was missing.

Dacron prepared to enter the Talent Void. To protect his delicate white skin against the damaging effects of this un-dimensional rift, he began rubbing on some SPF Factor Thirty Un-Block Lotion. He told Capt. Ricardo, "I will attempt to bring out at least two crewmembers every time I enter the void. On each trip, I will lose some of my own dimensionality. I hope to retain enough of it to enable me to keep entering the void until I have rescued everyone."

Dacron handed Ricardo a pocket-sized device and said, "This is a Dimensionality Meter. Please take a baseline reading on me at this time." Ricardo passed the meter in front of Dacron's chest and noted the reading: MULTIFA-CETED.

"Good luck, Dacron," Ricardo said solemnly. Dacron nodded and walked over to the void. With a crowbar, he pried open an entry point. He stepped over the crowbar and disappeared into nothingness.

The others waited as a minute passed, then two minutes, then three. Nothing happened. They began to fidget, anxious for even the most minor breakthrough to occur.

Suddenly the crowbar clattered to the floor as Dacron burst through the opening, dragging Commander Piker and Dr. Beverage Flusher with him. Piker and Flusher staggered and fell to the floor in a faint. The others rushed to help them.

"They are very simplistic at present," Dacron stated. He propped up Flusher's feet to improve circulation and began removing her boots. "Commander Piker has lost many of his charismatic quirks, and Doctor Flusher has regressed to physician-only status. However, since they were in the void for a limited time, they should recover quickly from their shallowness."

"Are they at risk of going into shock or anything?" Smirk asked. Piker's eyes were rolling back into his head, and his beard was slightly askew.

"That is a possibility," Dacron answered.

Crisco clicked his insignia communicator. "Crisco to Dr. Brassiere," he said. "Doctor, we need you in the guest quarters."

"I'm on my way, Com*mahn*der," came Brassiere's voice.

"How can you be 'on your way,' Brassiere?" Crisco retorted. He was obviously cranky from the tension of this mission. "I just asked you to come a millisecond ago. You couldn't possibly be on your way. If you were to say, 'I *will be* on my way,' I could see it, maybe. But don't tell me you're already on your way. Is that clear?"

There was a long pause. Finally Brassiere said, "I think so, Com*mahn*der. Perhaps I should bring along some extra *Vah*lium for you. Brassiere out."

Smirk propped up Piker's feet and began removing the boots as Dacron had done for Flusher, but Ricardo stopped him. "Wait, Captain," Ricardo said. "Commander Piker's foot odor is quite . . . quite . . . distinctive, shall we say. It's best not to be in the vicinity of his stockinged feet without a gas mask." Smirk dropped Piker's foot like a hot potato. Piker's ankle twisted as the heavy boot hit the floor, and he moaned.

As Dacron stepped back into the void, the others tended to Dr. Flusher. Smirk studied her pale face and announced, "I'll take care of Beverage. She probably needs mouth-to-mouth resuscitation." He gazed at her elegant lipline.

"Captain, *really*," chided Crisco, staring pointedly at Flusher's chest and shoulders, which rose and fell dramatically with each breath.

"Better safe than sorry," Smirk countered.

"We should probably wake them up," Crisco said. Dodo took the hint and shape-shifted into a bottle of smelling salts, waving himself under Flusher's nose. She awoke with a start.

"Doctor, how do you feel?" Crisco inquired.

"Flat," she answered. "Like I'm a doctor, and that's that."

Dodo wafted his smelling-salt self under Piker's nose. Piker's eyelids fluttered, but he remained unconscious, so Dodo became a pail of cold water and dumped himself over Piker's head. Piker shivered but still failed to come around. Finally Dodo shifted back into his doughy self and stared at Piker in exasperation.

Capt. Ricardo took on the challenge. He grasped his first officer's shoulders and shook him. "Commander Piker!" Ricardo said sharply. "Wilson! Can you hear me?" That failed to rouse Piker, so Ricardo made a fist and whomped Piker's jaw. "Wake up!" Ricardo shouted. He raised his arm over his head to get more momentum and struck Piker's face a second time.

Piker moaned and started to rouse himself. Ricardo slugged him again for good measure and was halfway through his next backswing when he noticed that the others were staring at him. He lowered his arm, admitting, "I've always wanted to do that."

Groaning, Piker propped himself up on his elbows and asked, "Where am I?"

"Dacron just rescued you from a Talent Void," Ricardo told him. "Your dimensionality level is low right now. Can you remember any other facets of your personality outside of your official duties?"

Piker shook his head.

Ricardo persisted, "How about playing your trombone? Playing poker? Playing around in Ten-Foreplay?"

"Uh-uh," Piker said. He grimaced and rubbed his temples. "Wait—there is something. Some athletic game. I think we play it in the HolidayDeck. It's called something like ... Parcheesi Squares, I think."

Dodo muttered to Crisco, "This multi-dimensional stuff is definitely overrated."

At that instant, Dacron, Mr. Smock and Dr. McCaw fell

Dodo became a pail of cold water and dumped
himself over Piker's head.

out of the void like exhausted marathon runners crossing the finish line. Smirk, Ricardo and Dodo went to the rescue of the newcomers, who seemed even more dazed than the first rescuees. "Dr. Brassiere, get here on the double!" Crisco yelled at the intercom.

"Just a moment, please, Com*mahn*der," Brassiere's voice replied. "I'm having trouble locating my box of Flintstone bandages."

"We don't need bandages!" Crisco said. "Bring some oxygen. We've got people passing out right and left."

Ricardo waved the Dimensionality Meter over Dacron and noted the readout: MILDLY COMPLEX. Ricardo observed, "You're starting to lose dimensionality, Dacron. Perhaps you should take a short rest and resume this rescue later on."

"I cannot do that, Captain," Dacron said. "Now that the rescue has begun, it must be finished promptly. This opening in the void will only remain for an hour or so. It is a simple law of physics."

"Ah, the beauty of physics," Ricardo said. "These phenomena keep everything so tidy. What's the official technobabble for this one? The Doppler Effect?" Dacron shook his head.

"Wait—I think we've used this before," Smirk said. He guessed, "The Gobbler Effect?"

"The Bubbler Effect?" Crisco chimed in.

Dacron shook his head, told them, "The Dramatic Effect," and popped back into the void. Within a few minutes he returned, dragging a comatose Zulu and Checkout by their epaulets.

Dr. Brassiere arrived and began tending to Mr. Smock, whose Vulture ears were drooping seriously. "Gosh, this is exciting!" Dr. Brassiere yipped. "Another brand-new frontier malady to contend with." He pressed a hippospray against Smock's neck, but Smock failed to respond. Ricardo passed his meter over Smock; it read SUPERFICIAL.

When Brassiere was unable to rouse Smock and the next

three unconscious patients he worked on, he moved over to Piker, who was already recovering on his own and would therefore be a more satisfying case.

As Dacron brought back still another pair of comatose crewmates—Yoohoo and Troit—and the others turned their attention to them, the confusion in the guest quarters heightened. No one noticed Dr. Brassiere helping Piker remove his boots.

Suddenly a horrible stench filled the room. Eyes watered, and people began coughing and gagging. Seeing that Piker's feet were exposed, Ricardo cried, "Good heavens!" and staggered over to his first officer. With remarkable dexterity borne of necessity, Ricardo placed the boots back on Piker's feet with one hand, holding his nose shut with the other hand.

The pungent odor lingered, threatening to overcome everyone standing in the guest quarters, but it did have the benefit of rousing the newly rescued crewmembers from their comas. They began dragging themselves toward the nearest exit. Smirk opened the door to the hallway, and Dodo pitched in by turning himself into a three-speed box fan to draw fresh air from outside.

Dr. Brassiere borrowed the Dimensionality Meter from Capt. Ricardo and passed it over Dr. Flusher's torso. Brassiere told her, "You seem to be coming around, Doctor."

"I think so, too," she said, grasping his forearm as he helped her sit up.

"It's all starting to come back to me," Flusher said. She continued clutching Brassiere's arm. "Besides my medical career, I've got a regular social routine. Every morning I have high tea with Captain Ricardo. . . . "

"I see," Brassiere said. "Well, now that you're feeling better, I'll just go on to the next patient—"

" . . . followed by another morning ritual," Beverage went on, "in which I do a stretching and flexibility workout with Counselor Troit. . . . "

"Oh?" Brassiere responded, feigning interest as he tried

to gently pry Flusher's fingers off his forearm.

"...and after that," Flusher said, hanging on to Brassiere even tighter, "I do my final morning ritual: gazing at a photograph of my son Westerly, my only child, my flesh and blood, who has set a galaxy-wide standard for dweebdom. That always sends me back to bed with a migraine."

"How very interesting," Brassiere said in a valiant attempt at politeness.

Flusher's eyes had taken on a desperate look. "I think I feel a migraine coming on now," she said. "You wouldn't happen to have any Migra-Ban tablets, would you?"

"I do indeed," Brassiere said. "In fact, I invented Migra-Ban."

Brassiere handed a bottle of the tablets to Flusher and remarked, "The drug company provides me with unlimited samples, as well as lots of other handy little thingamabobs with drug names printed on them." He began pulling doodads out of his pockets. "Here, would you like a pocket flashlight?" he offered. Flusher shook her head. "How about a lint remover? A needle threader? A nose-hair tweezer? A plastic pocket-sized rain bonnet?"

Dacron had rescued about two-thirds of the crewmembers from the void when Something Went Wrong.

After pushing Chief Engineer Snot by the buttocks to safety, Dacron staggered out after him and fell to the floor. Dr. Brassiere hovered over Dacron helplessly; he was totally unfamiliar with android physiology. The crewmate most familiar with Dacron's technology, Georgie LaForgery, was still trapped in the void. Even Dr. Flusher wasn't sure what to do as Dacron coughed and sputtered like a '79 Camaro on economy gasoline.

The other medical officer, Dr. McCaw, had been rescued earlier and was still lying on his back. Capt. Smirk shook his shoulder and said, "Wake up, Moans! It's a medical emergency."

"Arrgghh," Dr. McCaw growled. "Leave me alone. I feel awful."

"But a patient needs you," Smirk insisted. "You're the only one here who might be able to help him."

"For Pete's sake, Jim," McCaw crabbed, "I'm a doctor, not a doctor."

"What?" asked Smirk, bewildered and exasperated.

McCaw stared at the ceiling for a moment, then rubbed his hands over his face. "That didn't make sense," he admitted. "I guess I have no choice but to practice some medicine here." Smirk helped him to his feet.

It took McCaw just a few minutes to diagnose Dacron's problem—a clogged carburetor—and rig up a temporary fix so Dacron could finish the rescue. Dacron matter-of-factly mentioned that if everything didn't go perfectly for the rest of this mission, he and the others would be trapped in the void, and that by the time another rescue could be attempted, they'd have become so shallow as to be unfit for duty anywhere except the Sitcom Sector. Then he cheerily popped back into the rift.

Word quickly spread around the space station that the rescue was in jeopardy. This was a rare bit of genuine drama, and it drew people like ants to a discarded Sugar Daddy caramel sucker. Soon all of Cmdr. Crisco's inner circle plus a large crowd of gawkers were clustered in the guest quarters, staring at Dacron and the rescuees.

Dacron's strength was ebbing, and he could only bring people out one at a time. Whenever Dacron emerged from the void, Ricardo passed the Dimensionality Meter over him. Dacron's dimensionality was leaking out much more rapidly: within minutes he went from PEDESTRIAN to GIMMICKY to TRITE.

As the meter approached SHALLOW, Dacron began to resemble a permanent resident of the station. On one trip out of the void, he noticed Major Vera standing in the crowd and called to her, "We must keep Badger for Bridgeorans." The next time around, Dr. Brassiere was nearby, which prompted Dacron to make the Brassiere-like announcement that "This entire station is infected with the virus. Without an antidote, we're doomed."

The high drama unfolding before them—the poignancy of this android sacrificing his own talent to save the others from mediocrity—affected Crisco and his cronies so deeply that they somehow managed to transcend their standard responses.

Major Vera started out with her usual clichés of throwing a fit and then bawling, but gradually she got around to a new reaction. She became tense and fearful, and began biting her fingernails. Within a few minutes she had worked up to biting Yoohoo's fingernails, which were much longer and had been professionally manicured.

Dr. Brassiere stayed away from his two extremes of either professional detachment or naive overreaction. Instead, he felt guilty for failing to provide a cure for dullimia, which could have averted this crisis in the first place.

Security Chief Dodo began to empathize with Dacron. Suddenly Dodo realized that the android was a lot like him: a misunderstood loner with slicked-back hair and a deadpan face that glowed brighter than the full moon, like the Allen-Bradley clock tower at midnight.

Cmdr. Crisco, abandoning his usual manner of the conscientious leader with the weight of the world on his shoulders, bluntly admitted that he was sick of all this responsibility. He announced that if the rescue didn't turn out all right, he would take Joke back to Earth and pursue his secret dream of becoming a real estate broker.

Jazzy Fax, usually as frosty and slick as a blueberry Popsicle, lost her composure for a change. She began to cry, and when Major Vera tried to comfort her, Fax pushed Vera away and went into a corner to pout, her lower lip thrust out coquettishly.

Chief Bartender Quirk offered to take up a collection on behalf of the relatives of those still trapped. He swore on his mother's safe deposit box that all the money collected would go to the victims' families.

Crisco's son, Joke, and Quirk's nephew, Eggnog, seemed unusually muted as they faced this crisis. Eggnog pulled out a rosary he'd acquired while picking a tourist's pocket. The two boys started to say the rosary but couldn't remember most of the words. Smiles O'Brine offered to teach them, which reminded him of his brother, an Irish priest; and soon Smiles was weeping without shame as he recounted a sentimental story about the Auld Sod.

By the time Dacron pulled the last victim out of the void, the station regulars were mired in a swamp of sorrow, gratitude and guilt.

Dacron collapsed for a final time. Dr. McCaw checked him over and announced, "There's nothing space medicine can do for him now." Georgie LaForgery gave Dacron the once-over, then shook his head in defeat.

Ricardo knelt next to Dacron and passed the Dimensionality Meter over the android's chest. It registered below SUPERFICIAL.

Crisco crouched next to Ricardo and gazed at Dacron. "Is there any hope he'll rebound from this?" he murmured.

"I haven't the foggiest," Ricardo replied. "There's nothing more that we can do for him. It's all in the hands of— uh, forgive me. We're not supposed to say that."

Crisco replied, "You mean 'It's all in the hands of God'?" Ricardo winced.

"It's okay, Captain," Crisco continued. "The twenty-fourth-century gag order on religion has been suspended for the entire region of Badger."

"Well, that's a relief," Ricardo said. He added in a confidential tone, "Could you put me in touch with a holy person while we're here? It's been forty-three years since my last confession, and I've got a lot on my mind."

"I'll look into it," Crisco promised.

They returned their attention to the android at hand. Dacron still hadn't stirred. He was breathing, but otherwise he looked deader than dead, and the meter showed that his personality remained as flat as a day-old Pepsi.

Counselor Troit joined the senior officers. "Commander," she said to Crisco, "I'm reading strong mixed feelings among your people: anger, pity, sorrow, guilt, gratitude, despair, confusion, envy, jealousy, peevishness, disgust, wistfulness, rage, vengefulness, and nostalgia."

"Yes, Counselor," Crisco replied. "Terrifying, isn't it?"

"On the contrary," said Troit, "I think it's wonderful. Dacron's sacrifice wasn't in vain. Their emotional range has just increased one hundred and fifty percent."

9

The Play's
the Thing

IT WAS STILL thirty minutes to curtain, but already the Very Little Theater on Capt. Ricardo's *Endocrine* was full, and people were fighting over standing room in the back.

Ricardo's senior officers had gotten there first and hogged all the good seats. The second wave of people who had arrived were mostly from Smirk's ship. Crisco's people had come last and were squeezing into the remaining space. Some of them tried using their newly-acquired personality skills to charm their way into the few good seats still open near the front.

Major Vera approached Smock, eyeing the empty front-row chair between him and Capt. Ricardo. "So, Mr. Smock," she said conversationally, "I've heard that you Vultures can knock out opponents just by pinching them on the shoulder. Is that right?"

"That is correct, Major," Smock answered. Noticing Vera's covetous glance at the empty chair, Smock rested his arm protectively across the seatback.

"You think you could teach that pinch to me?" Vera asked. "I could use it the next time a fight breaks out among the senior officers in our Sloperations Command Center." She inched closer to the vacant spot.

Smock countered her move by setting his soft drink cup

on the chair seat. Though his face remained calm, his fingers on the cup betrayed slight nervousness, twiddling with the straw stuck in the plastic lid. "That would not be possible, Major," said Smock. "I have taken a solemn oath not to reveal the Vulture Pinch to a non-Vulture."

Sensing that this subtlety tack was getting her nowhere, Major Vera came right out with it: "Say, Smock, mind if I sit next to you?"

"I am sorry, Major," Smock said, "but Captain Ricardo has asked me to save this seat for Commander Crisco."

Vera stopped pretending to be sociable and switched to righteous indignation. "Oh, I get it," she retorted. "A Bridgeoran isn't good enough to sit in the front row, is that it?"

Vera's sudden flash of anger fascinated Smock, and as he studied how her face seemed to make a fist, he failed to notice Cmdr. Crisco approaching from the other side and being waved toward the empty seat by Ricardo. At the last second, Smock's peripheral vision registered Crisco's incoming buttocks, and he reflexively pulled his hand away; but the soda cup remained on the seat, and Crisco sat on it.

It took a couple of seconds for the impact to register. Crisco frowned slightly, realizing that something had happened yet not wanting to admit it, since doing something about it would mean giving up his precious front-row seat.

Ricardo noticed the shift in Crisco's expression. "Is something wrong, Commander?" he asked.

On Crisco's other side, Smock discreetly pulled out the squashed and dripping cup and placed it on the floor.

"Not really, Captain," Crisco replied, stoically ignoring the icy liquid wicking through the fabric under his thigh. "Why don't you tell me about this performance we're going to see?" he asked, hoping to distract Ricardo from this gaffe until the house lights went down and he could unobtrusively wring out his pants leg.

"Jolly good," Ricardo replied, obviously pleased to be

asked. "Well, you know how dull Dacron was when he finished rescuing everyone from the Talent Void."

Crisco nodded, recalling how deeply Dacron had been affected. While the others had gradually recovered their personalities, Dacron remained as flat as a hairdo squashed by a bicycle helmet.

"I knew there was one sure way to get Dacron back into shape," Ricardo continued. "On our ship, we have a saying: 'When the going gets tough, the tough get into the HolidayDeck and start goofing off.' So I assigned Dacron to use the HolidayDeck to stage a production of the Shakespearean play of his choice, playing all of the characters himself."

"And it worked?" Crisco asked.

"It did indeed," Ricardo said. "Dacron rose to the challenge. I've been watching his progress during rehearsals, and he's worked his way back from superficiality to complexity, perhaps even beyond where he was before.

"Tonight, he'll play one role live. He has recorded the other performances in a HolidayDeck program, and they'll be projected onstage during the performance," Ricardo explained. "Everyone you see onstage will be Dacron in one guise or another—though you'll swear they're played by a half-dozen or more people, since he's done such a superb job of delineating all the roles."

"Wonderful, Captain," Crisco said. "I hope my people on the space station can do even half that well with our own real selves. Dacron has given us a good start; now we need to keep developing our personalities."

"Perhaps you will," Ricardo said, "provided Starfreak Command starts sending you some non-clichéd missions."

Capt. Smirk, sitting on the other side of Ricardo, leaned over toward the two of them. "That was some call from Admiral Gogetter this morning, eh?" he inquired.

"It certainly was," Ricardo answered. "I've never before seen anyone paint a self-portrait, review his stock portfolio, eat a Mallo Cup, *and* play the concertina while talking on the Viewscreen."

"—And digging in the wastebasket, too," Crisco said, wrinkling his nose in disgust. "If that were my wastebasket and I'd accidentally thrown away something important, I'd call in a toxic waste cleanup team to look for it instead of diving in there myself."

"No, guys," Smirk said, "what I meant was, how about what Gogetter said during the call? Isn't it terrific?"

With a cheerleader's zeal, Smirk went on, "Think of it, Crisco. Word is getting around that your station has become less boring. Now that alien travel agencies have taken Geek Space Nine off their blacklist, tourist trade is already picking up. And Ricardo and I will get to keep our ships."

Crisco agreed, "It has turned out better than I would've dreamed. Let's hope that that patch over the slow leak in the Talent Void will hold up over the long run, so my people don't start losing dimensionality again."

"Time will tell," Ricardo remarked.

Lt. Jazzy Fax stood in front of them, scanning the rows for a seat. "Oh, Jazzy, my sweet," Capt. Smirk lilted, "there's a place for you here." Seeing no vacant seats nearby, she gave him a puzzled look. Smirk finished his invitation: " . . . on my lap."

Fax frowned at him. "Sorry, Captain," she said. "I'm not interested in pursuing our relationship. You're not deep enough for me. Anyway, I'm giving up on romance for a while."

"Oh, really?"

"Yes," Fax continued with childlike solemnity. "Now that I'm multidimensional, my social life must take a back seat. In my free time, I'm going to pursue some worthwhile form of higher education." She wrinkled her forehead prettily, speculating, "Maybe I'll respond to that ad I keep seeing in the back pages of *Cosmopolitan* for a correspondence course in fashion merchandising."

Dr. Brassiere approached her eagerly. "Lieutenant Fax—"

"I'm sorry, Julio," she interrupted. "Now that I'm multidimensional, I'm afraid I must break off our relationship."

"What relationship?" Dr. Brassiere said. "Every time I say hello to you, you fall asleep."

"That's right," Fax said, "and I simply don't have time for those pleasantries anymore."

"Well, gee," Brassiere said, "I just wanted to know if you'd like to watch the show with me."

"You've found some empty seats?" Fax asked.

"No, not—not exactly," Brassiere stuttered. Fax's interest turned to skepticism as Brassiere started backpedaling. "I mean, no, not actual seats. But I've volunteered to serve as the house doctor for the evening, in case any emergencies come up. So I get to watch from backstage, and I was hoping you'd like to stand with me."

"Oh, boy, a chance to be on my feet on a dusty stage for two hours, watching the performers from the wrong side," Fax said sarcastically. "Be still, my beating heart." She pranced away from Brassiere.

He gazed after her wistfully. "Gosh, her dimensionality is coming along *mah*velously," he observed aloud to himself. "I've never known her to be so rude."

Off to one side, Guano and Quirk were hurriedly setting up a makeshift popcorn stand. "This is a great idea," Guano said. "I only wish you'd come up with it sooner so we could've gotten an early start."

"I didn't think of it till I walked in here and saw this theater setup," Quirk said. "Then it hit me: this is just like a movie house. And what's the most profitable part of that business? The popcorn angle."

Guano poured kernels into the huge metal popper. "I hear Dacron is staging a comedy," she said. "Popcorn sells well during a comedy, right?"

"Right," Quirk affirmed. "Running this concession will

be like finding gold. We take five cents' worth of popcorn, add a little heat and air and butter, and *voilà!* We sell it for three-seventy-five a carton. I love this stuff," he added, "though I don't eat it myself. It tends to get stuck between my teeth."

"I could see how you'd have a problem," Guano sympathized, gazing at Quirk's tooth structure, which looked like a multi-denture collision. "Orthodontists must love you Ferengis."

"Yeah, us and Kringles," said Quirk.

The lone Kringle in the audience, Security Officer Wart, squirmed in his chair. Capt. Ricardo had forced all of his senior officers to attend this performance. Wart had come early to claim an aisle seat, but now he regretted it since he was feeling restless. He hated to sit in one place for more than a few minutes.

Crisco's security officer, Dodo, sat next to Wart. Dodo had made a seat for himself in the aisle by shape-shifting his rear end into a chair form. "Will you stop fidgeting?" Dodo fussed at Wart.

"I cannot help it," Wart said. "The theater bores me. Especially comedies."

"How can you be bored?" Dodo said. "The performance hasn't even started." Wart grumbled in his deep, powerful bass; the seats around him shook slightly.

"I never let myself be bored," Dodo said. "I find ways to amuse myself." Wart grunted.

"Here, I'll show you," Dodo continued. He dissolved into a blob of Silly Putty, then began shape-shifting in imitation of objects lying around on the floor: a crumpled playbill, an empty box of candy, a soggy Kleenex tissue.

"Not bad," Wart admitted.

Dodo shifted into his next imitation—a wad of discarded bubble gum—and sat on the floor looking pink and wrinkly and cerebral-cortex-like.

Zulu and Checkout stood in the aisle next to Wart, scanning the seats farther down the row. "Excuse me,"

Checkout said, pointing to a pair of empty chairs. "Is anyone sittingk in dose seats?"

"What does it look like?" Wart countered.

Zulu and Checkout glanced at each other and shrugged. "I guess that means they're free," Zulu said. "Excuse us, please, Lieutenant," Zulu said, stepping nimbly past Wart. Checkout followed, swinging his boot carefully over Wart and landing squarely on Dodo the Gumwad. A muffled squeak emerged from beneath Checkout's foot.

"Did you hear sometink?" Checkout asked Zulu. Zulu shook his head and continued making his way toward the empty seats. Checkout persisted, "It sounded just like dat scientist in da movie *Da Fly*," he said, "in dat part vhere he gets caught in a spiderveb and says 'Hellllp meee, hellllp meee.' "

Zulu narrowed his eyes at Checkout and leaned over to sniff his breath, wondering if Checkout had been nipping at the vodka tonight.

They reached their seats. "Dere's dat noise again!" Checkout exclaimed. "It came from down here some-vhere." He lifted his foot, and suddenly Dodo popped back into humanoid shape with a waffle-sole pattern imprinted on his face. Dodo's cheeks reddened with embarrassment, heightening the zigzag lines.

Dodo made a quick exit, stumbling past the knees of the people between him and the aisle. "Excuse me . . . pardon me . . . coming through," he mumbled.

A few rows up, Chief Engineers Snot and LaForgery sat with Smiles O'Brine, the fix-it guru of Geek Space Nine. "I have to admit," said Georgie, "this is the first play I've seen in years."

"If we weren't required to attend, would the three of us be here at all?" O'Brine asked rhetorically.

The other two shook their heads. "You're right abou' that, lad," Mr. Snot said. "The only use I have for fiction is makin' up excuses to tell th' captain when th' engine isn't worrrkin'."

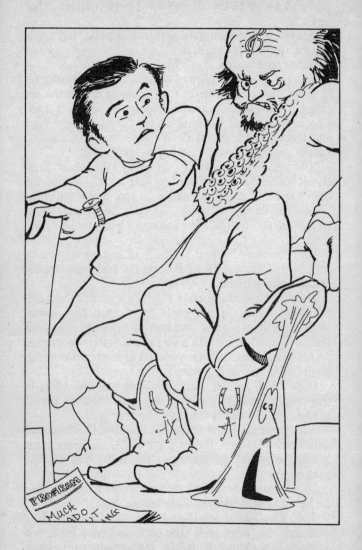

"Did you hear sometink?"

"The thing is," said Georgie, "we engineers live with drama every day—writing up specifications for pipes, drawing flowcharts, consulting tables of numbers—so it's hard to sit in an audience trying to get worked up over the imaginary problems of some artificial characters."

"Engineers and the theater don't mix," O'Brine stated. "You can lead a geek to drama, but you can't make him think it."

Farther ahead, in the aisle on the right, Joke and Eggnog stood on tiptoe and scanned the crowd. "Do you see them?" Joke asked.

"Not yet," said Eggnog, craning his neck to look over the people milling around them. "Wait—there they are. I think there are two sets open in front of them, too."

"Perfect," said Joke. "We can turn around and talk to them whenever the show gets dull."

"Don't you two think Counselor Troit and Officer Yoo-hoo are a little old for you?" Westerly Flusher asked pointedly.

Joke and Eggnog had been trying to lose Westerly all evening, without success. Wart's son, Smartalecsander, had disappeared a moment before, promising them he had a plan to get Westerly out of the way.

"Hey, Westerly, aren't you supposed to be somewhere else tonight?" Joke said.

"Yeah," Eggnog taunted, "don't you have a toilet-training lesson right now? Or is it a meeting of Thumb-Suckers Anonymous?"

Smartalecsander reappeared from the crowd and sidled up to Joke and Eggnog. "It's all set," he muttered to the two older boys. "You guys owe me three bars of gold-pressed laudanum for this." He turned toward Westerly. "Hey, Wes," Smartalecsander said, "I found us two really good seats. Let's go before somebody else takes them."

"Neat-o!" Westerly exclaimed. He followed Smartalecsander to the rear of the theater, where a door opened onto a stairwell. Smartalecsander climbed the steps with Westerly coming up after him.

"The seats are in the balcony," Smartalecsander said. As they reached the landing, where the stairs turned toward the front of the theater, he noticed that Commander Piker had followed them through the doorway. "Uh, c'mon," Smartalecsander said. "We hafta hurry. There's only a few seats left." He pulled Westerly's sleeve.

"Hey, you two," called Piker. "Where do you think you're going?"

Westerly stopped, and Smartalecsander tugged at his arm. "Come on!"

Westerly looked down the stairwell. "But Commander Piker is—"

"Never mind him!" Smartalecsander said. "He wants to skip ahead of us and get the best seat. But we were here first. Let's go!"

For a moment, Westerly was like a lab rat caught in a classic approach/avoidance conflict. Would he defy Piker's authority, appear cool to Smartalecsander, and claim a good balcony seat? Or would he be his usual goody-goody self and do whatever an adult told him to?

For once, the need to be hip won out. Westerly clambered up the stairs with Smartalecsander.

Smartalecsander was the first to reach the door at the top. He swung it open and held it for Westerly. "After you," he said.

Westerly stepped over the threshold onto what appeared to be a carpeted balcony and immediately plunged downward. Smartalecsander held onto the doorknob and peered over the edge. Down on the first floor, Westerly was sprawled on his back across two empty seats.

There was much confusion as people around Westerly recovered from their shock and stood up to help. Smartalecsander saw that Westerly had landed on the seats Joke and Eggnog coveted, right in front of Counselor Troit and

Officer Yoohoo. "Oh, man," Smartalecsander whined. "There goes my commission."

Cmdr. Piker was closing in, so Smartalecsander shut the door halfway and stood guarding it.

Piker staggered up the last few steps, clutching the handrail. The climb had left him gasping for air like a sumo wrestler at high altitude. "You kids . . ."—he huffed and puffed—"shouldn't be . . . up here. The HolidayDeck's solid-matter buffer . . . isn't working right." He swallowed, wiped his brow, and added, "That balcony looks real . . . but there's nothing there."

"Sure there is," Smartalecsander piped up. "I fixed it."

"You did?" Piker asked.

"Sure, just a few minutes ago. Westerly's already sitting in one of the best spots," Smartalecsander said. "Better hurry before all the seats are taken. I think I hear some more people coming up the stairs." He held the door for Piker, who staggered over to the balcony entrance.

"Thanks, kid," Piker said. "You know, I used to think you were really a pain in the butt, but maybe you're okay after all."

Smartalecsander smiled wickedly. Piker stepped onto the illusion of a balcony and took the plunge.

Down below, as Troit and Yoohoo hovered over Westerly, somebody yelled "Look out!" The two women looked up, then reflexively jumped back as they saw Piker dropping toward them like a grand piano that had gotten away from the movers.

Westerly was still draped across two theater seats, and Piker landed on him with all the force of a senior officer with way too many Kringle ten-course meals to his credit. Bystanders cringed at the sickening *cr-r-aaaack* in which the flattening of Westerly mingled with the splintering of a wooden armrest.

"Is there a doctor in the house?" Troit called.

The on-call physician for the night, Dr. Brassiere, was backstage blabbing to Dacron as the android applied his

Piker stepped onto the illusion of a balcony and
took the plunge.

makeup. " . . . Not only did I find an antidote for the plague on Mucus-9," Brassiere said, "but I patented the formula and sold it for a tidy profit."

"I see," said Dacron, too polite to tell Brassiere that he was getting in the way of preparations for the performance. In fact, the distraction had caused Dacron to smear some of his makeup, which now had to be removed and re-done. "Doctor," Dacron asked, "would you please hand me that jar of kerosene?"

Back in the audience, Dr. Flusher stood on her chair and stared toward the back of the theater, just in time to see Piker climbing slowly out of the crash site. She realized that the call for a doctor was on behalf of her son, Westerly. "Oh my gosh!" Flusher shrieked. "Westerly! I'm coming! I'm coming!"

"Mommmmmyyyy!" Westerly cried, staring at the splintered armrest sticking up through his abdomen and wondering whether 24th-century medicine had developed a cure for this one.

Dr. McCaw was sitting next to Flusher, and she grabbed him by his jacket. "You're coming with me, McCaw," Flusher said. "You take care of Commander Piker while I work on Westerly."

"For crying out loud," McCaw complained, "don't I ever get an evening off?" Flusher shot him such an evil look that he rose and followed her up the aisle, still complaining: "If it's not one thing, it's another. Last month that woman 'had' to deliver her baby just as I was heading out to the golf course. A week ago some patient with third-degree phaser wounds interrupted my work on my coin collection. I'm going to get out of general medicine and into dermatology. There's no such thing as an emergency zit."

Just as Flusher and McCaw approached the scene of the accident, the house lights dimmed. "Hey, how are we supposed to work under these conditions?" McCaw demanded.

Onstage, Dr. Brassiere appeared in front of the curtain

and stepped into the spotlight. "Ladies and gentlemen," Brassiere began, "it's my pleasure to introduce—"

"We need more light!" Flusher called from the rear of the house.

"Turn the lights back up!" McCaw hollered.

Brassiere squinted into the spotlight. "Say, could you people hold it down back there?" he asked. "We've got a show to put on. Now, as I was saying," he continued, adjusting his collar importantly, "it's my great pleasure to introduce one of the premier theatrical talents of our sector, Lieutenant Commander Dacron. As you all know, Dacron recently saved a good number of Starfreak officers from dullimia, and as you'll see from this performance, he himself has recovered completely and has a full emotional range at his disposal."

"That's true," said Cmdr. Crisco, turning around to speak to co-workers who were sitting or standing near him. "Watch him closely. You might learn something."

Dr. Brassiere held up a sheet of paper and said, "Dacron has asked me to make this announcement." Brassiere read Dacron's message aloud: " 'For my one-android production, I have chosen the Shakespearean play which best represents the fuss Starfreak Command makes over this space station: *Much Ado About Nothing.*' "

Hearing several members of the audience chuckle, Brassiere peered out into the house and muttered, "I don't get it."

He crumpled up the paper and threw it away, concluding, "And so, may I present to you: Lieutenant Commander Dacron!"

Epilogue
The Revelation of the Audience

1 Now when the Network opened the first seal, I heard the voice say, "Watch!" [2]And I saw, and behold, a white horse, and seven heroes clad in white and wearing white hats, and they went out conquering all the bad guys of space.

3 When the second seal was opened, I heard the voice say, "Watch!" [4]And out came another band of heroes, a little more neurotic perhaps but nevertheless right-minded, and they went out to explore space.

5 Then the third seal was opened, and again I heard the voice say, "Watch!" [6]And behold, where the emperors' new clothes were supposed to be, I saw only nakedness. [7]And the voice said, "Great, isn't it?!" [8]I replied, "But they're naked!" [9]The voice answered, "No, they are not naked. They are the wave of the future. You're just not giving them a chance." [10]But those of the third wave sensed that they were lacking, and they tried making up for it with much weeping and wailing and gnashing of teeth.

11 Then the stage curtain was opened, and behold, a pale horse, and a pale rider, very pale, for his name was Dacron. [12]And he proclaimed, "I will rescue these characters from their naked predicament, but please under-

stand that I cannot continue doing this forever."

13 "We understand, O Dacron," cried those of the third wave. [14]"But tell us, what is our motivation?"

15 And he said, "You must work that out for yourselves. [16]But be quick about it. [17]For behold, the days are coming when yours will be the only new stories, and if you leave the Wrekkies unsatisfied, they shall go mad."

18 Thus stands the story that still has not reached its end.